# MATTHEW RIEF

# HUNTED IN THE KEYS

## A Logan Dodge Adventure

**Florida Keys Adventure Series**
**Volume 2**

This book is a work of fiction. Names, characters, businesses, places, events and incidents are either the products of the author's imagination or used in a fictitious manner. Any resemblance to actual persons, living or dead, or actual events is purely coincidental.

**Logan Dodge Adventures**

Gold in the Keys
(Florida Keys Adventure Series Book 1)

Hunted in the Keys
(Florida Keys Adventure Series Book 2)

Revenge in the Keys
(Florida Keys Adventure Series Book 3)

Betrayed in the Keys
(Florida Keys Adventure Series Book 4)

Redemption in the Keys
(Florida Keys Adventure Series Book 5)

If you'd like to receive my newsletter to get updates on upcoming books and special deals, you can sign up on my website:

matthewrief.com

# MAPS

Florida Keys
HOMESTEAD
KEY WEST
MARATHON

Texas Rock
Brilliant Shoal
Middle Key
East Key
Hospital Key
Loggerhead Key
Fort Jefferson on Garden Key
Bush Key
White Shoal
Long Key
Dry Tortugas
National Park

# ONE

Everglades National Park, Florida
Summer 2008

A soft breeze whistled through the tall sawgrass in the cool morning air. It was the only sound to be heard for miles, other than the squishing of mud under the soles of our boots as we trekked through the swamp. The distant sun was just starting to peek over the eastern horizon, illuminating the sky enough for us to switch off our flashlights and stow them inside our backpacks.

The three of us were spread out as we searched, with Jack Rubio thirty feet to my right and Scott Cooper thirty feet to my left. This allowed us to cover more ground as we hunted the elusive Burmese python, which had invaded the Everglades and had been multiplying dangerously for the past two decades. Jack, a good friend of mine since I was young, was born and bred in Southern Florida. A real-deal conch and the son of conchs back three generations. His curly blond hair flapped in the breeze beneath a blue snapback as he moved effortlessly through the difficult terrain just downwind of me.

I'd met Scott Cooper back when I was serving in the Navy. He had been the division officer of my Special Forces unit, and when he'd gotten out as a lieutenant commander, he'd gone into politics. Now he was in his first six-year term as a Senator representing the state of Florida. I hadn't seen him much since we'd struck Aztec gold a few months earlier at Neptune's Table, just south of the Marquesas Keys. I guess he'd finally gotten sick of life in Washington and needed to add a little adventure to his life, if only for a couple of days.

"Freeze!" Scott said, holding up his left hand, which was clenched into a fist. He was wearing a black bandana over the bottom half of his face and a faded Florida Marlins ball cap. He glanced at Jack and me, pointed two fingers at his focused eyes, then pointed ahead of him at a portion of the swamp where a narrow muddy channel met a thick patch of sawgrass.

I kept my body motionless and drew my gaze to where he was pointing. Slithering slowly across the water and leaving thin ripples in its wake was a young python, probably about six feet long. Their dark camouflaged bodies make them difficult to spot in the swamp, especially since most of their body is underwater and they usually hang out in thick underbrush. It's only when they're disturbed that they move out of hiding and become more visible to the naked eye.

Scott moved in closer, raised his Remington 870 shotgun up against his shoulder, and fired off a number four buckshot. The loud explosion boomed across the quiet swamp, echoing for miles as the twenty or so .24-inch lead balls slammed into the head of the unsuspecting python at over twelve hundred feet per second. Water, mud, and pieces of grass flew into the air. Blood pooled out from the python's head, and Scott cocked his shotgun and fired off another shell for good measure, causing the snake to struggle for a few seconds before going limp in the water.

"Hell yeah!" Jack shouted. "That's five for the day already."

Scott moved in, covering the sixty feet or so, and grabbed the python with a pair of Tomahawk snake tongs, then dragged it through the water towards us.

"Keep looking," Scott said. "I have a feeling there's more nearby."

Moving past us, he headed back towards our airboat, which was tied off to a line of mangroves a quarter of a mile west of us. I smiled and nodded at Scott, then took a step forward, scanning the swamp once more.

I glanced over at Jack and shook my head. "I had no idea they were such a problem here." Though Jack had hunted python in the Everglades many times before, this was my first time. I'd heard about the problem before but only realized its extent after seeing it firsthand.

Jack laughed. "Yeah, the buggers have no predators. Well, other than us they don't." He grinned.

While we'd cruised north along the Florida Keys on my forty-eight-foot Baia Flash, Jack had told me all about how the python had come to live in the Glades. In 1992, Hurricane Andrew had made landfall in Southern Florida. It was one of the worst hurricanes Florida had seen in recent memory, and it was so powerful that it had ruined large structures, including a private reptile-breeding facility near the Everglades. Following the storm, the zookeepers realized that they were missing many of their large reptiles, including Burmese pythons. The massive snakes thrived in the humid, swampy landscape of the Everglades, which was eerily similar to their native land of Southeast Asia. A female python can lay up to one hundred eggs at a time and live up to twenty years of age. With no predators in the Everglades, the Burmese python had become one of the worst invasive species in history. It was believed that over a hundred thousand of them lived in Southern Florida.

Moving through the patch of sawgrass, we came to another stretch of mud that was covered in about six inches of murky water. I advanced slowly through the mud and water, my hip boots sinking down enough to cover my knees at times. In my hands, I gripped my Winchester 1300, which was known for its fast-cycling pump action that made it ideal for hunting. Just like Scott, I'd loaded mine up with number four buckshot, a slug effective at longer ranges and powerful enough to take down a large deer with one well-placed shot.

After about five minutes of trekking, we'd made it about a football field from where Scott had taken down his snake. Jack and I moved quietly, swept up in the thrill of the hunt. A strong gust of Caribbean wind came out of nowhere, causing the blades of grass to dance and forming tiny whitecaps on the surface of the water. A moment later, I saw movement just a few feet in front of my boots, beneath a row of cattail plants and a cluster of lily pads. It was dark and it was huge, seemingly too big to be a python. I froze in place as the slow movements of the massive reptile appeared closer beneath the rippling waves. I held my breath as it slithered just a few inches from my right boot, its body camouflaged by the murky water and lily pads.

The first rule of python hunting is to never let the big ones get close. Realizing that I'd broken the first rule without even noticing, I gripped my shotgun, pulled it up snug against my right shoulder, and took aim. Jack froze thirty feet away from me as I fired off three slugs in succession, riddling the python's massive body with lead balls that exploded into its skin, sending out streams of blood. It tried to slither away, its body thrashing and splashing as it struggled its way through the swamp. Stepping towards it and seeing its head appear for the first time, I fired off two more shells, both of them hitting their target. Water splashed high into the air as its head disappeared from view. My eyes grew wide as I saw the python from head to tail for the first time. It was the biggest snake I'd ever seen, and I estimated that it was at least fifteen feet long.

Reaching swiftly for the Condor machete sheathed to my belt, I splashed through the water and gripped the struggling python by the slender part of its body a few slimy feet down from its head. Its muscles twitched as it tried to wrap its scales around me like I was lunch waiting to be crushed in its grasp. I grunted, reared back my machete, then slashed it fiercely through the humid air. The newly sharpened blade cut into the python's neck, slicing it in half and turning the water dark red. The python's enormous body went limp in the water just beside the patch of thick sawgrass as I turned to face Jack, my bloody machete raised triumphantly over my head.

"Jeez, bro, this monster's gotta be over sixteen feet! And it'll easily tip the scale at over a buck fifty." Jack ran over beside me and stood in awe of the massive reptile lying dead at my feet. "I've never seen one so big. Wait until the warden gets ahold of this. He'll probably want a picture for the paper."

I took a moment to admire my kill, then went to work. Grabbing a length of nylon rope, I tied it around the python's dead body, then wrapped it around my shoulder. "We gotta get it back to the airboat first," I replied, grinning.

It took both of us hauling the rope to move the snake through the water. It was difficult work dragging it through the mud, water, and grass, and the going was slow. We kept our eyes peeled and our guns ready for an alligator foolish enough to try and snatch our kill, but we both knew that it wasn't likely. Pythons in the Everglades were notorious for swallowing alligators, even large ones, whole.

"Damn, Logan," Scott said, meeting us halfway to where we'd tied off the airboat. "You always have to one-up me, don't you?"

I shrugged. "Competitive nature, I suppose. But the day's still young."

Jack laughed, shaking his head. "We won't see another like this one. No way. This has got to be the biggest snake ever caught in the Everglades. I'd be willing to bet money on it."

It was much easier with all three of us, and within ten minutes, we reached the airboat, with its grassy camo-painted hull, then curled up the snake and hauled its slimy body up onto the deck. It was too big to fit in the fish holding tank, so we coiled it up on the bow. The airboat we were using was a twenty-foot-by-eight-foot Air Ranger that sat up to six people comfortably and was propelled by a one-thousand-horsepower engine, which drove the large fan to propel it over the water at speeds up to seventy miles per hour.

A common sight in the Everglades, airboats have been the transportation of choice for people living there for decades. Perfect for the swampy landscape, they're fast and can operate in just a few inches of water due to their flat-bottomed hulls and no working parts underneath or on the waterline. It was a good thing we'd chosen one with so much power because by the end of the day, we probably had over six hundred pounds of dead snakes all told.

We spent a few more hours hunting a single-mile radius around the airboat and killed two more pythons, though neither were anywhere close to as big as the monster I'd taken down. By 1100, the tropical sun was almost directly above us, its rays burning down and driving the humid air up past ninety degrees. There was a swift and steady breeze, but it wasn't enough to keep us cool. We'd been downing gallons of chilled water from the cooler on the airboat but knew that it was time to call it a day. Besides, the airboat couldn't handle too much more, what with the three of us, our gear and the eight snakes we'd bagged.

I untied a rope lashed to a nearby mangrove branch, then shoved the boat out into a shallow channel and jumped aboard. Jack sat in the pilot's seat and, starting up the loud, colossal engine, he brought the massive metal fan to life and we began to move forward. We each grabbed and donned small foam earplugs, as well as over-the-ear protection, as the sounds from the fans can exceed a hundred decibels, which is the equivalent of being in the front row at a rock concert.

"Hold on," Jack yelled as he brought the boat into a larger body of water, his left hand gripping the metal steering rod with a firm grip as he pushed down on the throttle pedal with his right foot. The massive blades spun ferociously, rocketing us over the shallow swampland at over forty knots. The noise was loud even with the double hearing protection, like sticking your ear right up to a house fan, and the powerful wind beat against our faces. I held on to the metal handrail and pressed my body back into the seat behind me.

Looking out over the seemingly endless marshes, I marveled at the never-ending fields of sawgrass and cypress trees rising up out of the flat swampland in the distance. I thought about how amazing the place really was. The contrast between it and the tropical paradise of the Florida Keys always left me astonished. I'd been to the Everglades a few times before, deep into the heart of it, where not a lot of people had seen. I'd gone on camping trips with my dad, who'd taught me about life in the swamp, and being back there brought a smile to my face as I remembered those good times.

We cruised through Whitewater Bay, a massive body of water that reached all the way to Ponce de Leon Bay and the Gulf of Mexico to the west, heading south towards the opening into Tarpon Creek. Just as we were flying through the creek and into Coot Bay, Jack eased back on the gas pedal unexpectedly. Looking ahead, I didn't see anything in front of us. It was practically a straight shot across the bay and into Flamingo Channel.

I looked at Jack questioningly. "What's up, man?

You see something?" I glanced at my shotgun, which was bungee-strapped to the railing beside me, making sure that it was within arm's reach just in case.

"You see that?" he replied, his head tilted and his eyes looking out over the port side of the airboat. Scott and I both looked out that direction and, squinting and focusing my eyes, I saw a dark object far off in the sky.

Suddenly, Jack killed the engine and removed his hearing protection. Scott and I both did the same, and the three of us heard the unmistakable sound of helicopter rotors spinning through the air, growing louder each second as the aircraft headed towards us. I'd heard the sound so many times in my life. Usually it meant that we were being picked up following a mission, but sometimes it was a sound you didn't want to hear.

I reached for the monocular in the front pocket of my backpack and looked off in the direction of the chopper. It was approaching from the north, and I knew instantly that it wasn't a Coast Guard helicopter. It was dark gray, a pretty good size, and it was flying low and fast straight for us.

Handing the monocular to Jack, I said, "What do you think?"

He took a look and replied, "There are only a few tourist helicopters that run flights around this part of the Glades. And that sure as hell isn't one of them. It's far too big."

Instinctively, I reached for my Sig, which was strapped to my holster in the main compartment of my backpack.

Scott put his hand on me and shook his head. "It's for me."

My eyes grew wide. "Are you sure?" He nodded

and I added, "Why would they fly all the way out here in the middle of nowhere to get to you?"

He shrugged. "I don't know, but it can't be good."

As I watched it fly closer, I realized that it was a Sikorsky VH-3D Sea King, the same make and model used by the president, and it was painted dark blue and white. Jack told us to put our ear protection back on, then started the engine back up and maneuvered the airboat towards a patch of dry land off our starboard side that was big and flat enough for the large helicopter to land on.

Within thirty seconds, the helicopter was right over our heads, descending slowly. The wind from its blades blew the grass flat below it and caused the muddy water to stir. We shielded our faces as the pilot brought her down softly, its tires making contact with the ground and its blades slowing slightly. After a few seconds, the side door slid open and a small staircase folded out. Scott and I hopped out of the airboat and waded through the muddy shore onto dry land as two guys wearing nice suits appeared in the doorway and walked down the steps. One of the guys stopped at the base of the stairs, but the other continued until he was standing right in front of us.

"Senator Cooper," the guy said, loud enough to be heard over the roar of the helicopter blades. He looked to be in his early forties and was about my height, with a bald head and dark-rimmed sunglasses. "I need you to get on the helicopter right now. We have a situation."

Scott stepped closer to him. "What kind of situation?"

The guy started to open his mouth, then tilted his head and looked at me skeptically. "The classified kind," he said sternly.

"Logan was Special Forces. He's been involved in more classified situations than you ever will, Kurt."

The guy stared at Scott, seeming offended by his words. After a moment's pause, he motioned back towards the helicopter. "Regardless, specifics are on a need-to-know basis. I need you to get on the helicopter right now, sir."

Scott turned, walked back to the airboat and grabbed his backpack. "I'm sorry to cut the trip short, guys."

"All good, bro," Jack said. "It was a good time. I hope it's nothing too serious."

"Me too," he replied.

"Call us if you need help with anything," I said. Then, glancing at the bald guy in the suit, I added, "Be careful."

He smiled, patted us both on the back, then moved swiftly for the helicopter. He and Baldy met up with the other suit at the base of the stairs, and the three of them climbed up and disappeared into the main section of the helicopter. Seconds later, the stairs rose up behind them and the blades roared back to life, thrusting the helicopter up into the air. Within a minute it was heading north, disappearing into the horizon.

I looked over at Jack, and he just laughed. "What the hell was that about?" he said.

"Who knows? Looked pretty important."

Jack thought it over a moment as I shoved off the airboat, my boots sinking into the muddy water.

"Well, I say we should head over to the Flamingo Marina for lunch," he said. "Could be some nutcase has finally decided to drop a bomb. I'd hate to face the end of the world on an empty stomach."

# TWO

I took over the controls and maneuvered the airboat across Coot Bay and into Flamingo Channel, a long, narrow stretch of water that reaches all the way to the Flamingo Marina and the Everglades National Park Headquarters at the very bottom of Florida's mainland. Though it was tempting to push her to her limits and see what she had speed-wise, I knew that manatees swam in those waters. The last thing I wanted was to hit one of the large, peaceful creatures, so I held the airboat steady at about twenty knots and kept a watchful eye on the water ahead of us. Often referred to as sea cows, manatees have been an endangered species for ten years, mainly due to accidents involving unobservant and reckless boaters.

After navigating roughly three miles through the channel, I saw the two docks extending out along the boat ramp and the green metal roof of the Flamingo Marina's main building. Slowing down, I navigated the airboat towards the docks and spotted an alligator sprawled out near the shore, its rough, jagged body baking in the afternoon sun. Near the middle of the water, I saw two manatees swimming blissfully along the shore, bobbing their large circular bodies up and down.

I pulled the airboat up alongside a small cypress-planked dock, then killed the engine as Jack tied us off. Moving down the dock towards the shore, we headed for the office, a white building that housed the main office as well as a small restaurant. After checking in with the owner of the airboat, a man who Jack had known since he was young, we headed down a concrete path towards where the Baia was moored at one of the docks on the ocean side of the compound. Climbing aboard, we hosed down our muddy boots, then changed into casual attire and headed over to the ranger station a few hundred feet away.

The ranger station and visitor center were two rather large cement buildings, painted bright pink just like a flamingo. There used to be a restaurant there as well, but Hurricanes Katrina and Wilma had done serious damage to part of the building just a few years ago in 2005. The decision had been made never to repair the restaurant, and it still looked torn to hell to that day. Fortunately, the ranger station portion had been repaired.

Jack and I walked up the stairs and entered through a pair of glass doors. A small bell rang as we walked inside, and a friendly woman in her fifties greeted us behind a small desk.

"What can I do for you gentlemen?" she said. "You two looking for information on the area?"

As I walked up to the counter, I saw that it was mostly bare aside from a computer monitor and a donation jar with the black Wounded Warrior emblem printed on it. Glancing at her nameplate, I realized it was the same woman I'd talked to on the phone the day before when I'd reserved the moorage for the Baia.

"Martha, it's good to meet you," I said, holding out my hand. "My name is Logan Dodge, and this is Jack Rubio."

As the three of us shook hands, she said, "Ah, yes. The owner of the forty-eight Baia. It sure is a beautiful boat."

"Thanks. Look, we just got back from hunting pythons in the northern marshes of Whitewater. Is there any way you could get a warden on the line and have him head over this way? We just need to have them weighed and turned in."

"We've been in contact with Mitch Ross," Jack said, mentioning the name of the head warden in the Everglades. "He knows that we're here and should be expecting a call."

"I'm afraid Mitch is up north for a few days," she said. "A family emergency took him out of the state just this morning. But we have someone here filling in for him." She reached for a radio lying on the desk in front of her. "Just give me a second and I'll let him know to head over."

After calling the guy on her radio, she said he was on his way over and shouldn't be more than a few minutes. We thanked her and used the time to walk back to the docks and haul the snakes from our airboat onto the shore using a large metal cart. Once there, we straightened them out on a patch of grass beside the ranger station and covered them with a large tarp. Being summertime, the place wasn't very busy, but the few people walking around the grounds stared in awe at the massive snakes. Once the pythons were off, we grabbed the rest of our gear, loaded it onto the Baia and sprayed down the airboat with a nearby hose to clean off all of the snake blood.

About ten minutes after we talked to Martha, a white park ranger SUV with tinted windows and a green stripe down the side pulled into the driveway. A guy who looked like he was in his early twenties stepped out and walked over to us. He was wearing the typical park ranger outfit, including khaki shorts and one of those goofy-looking but functional round hats.

"I'm guessing you two are Mr. Rubio and Mr. Dodge?" the young man said, holding his hand out to us. He was a tall, skinny kid with short brown hair and a tanned baby face. "My name is Ryan Cody. I'm filling in for Mitch for a few days."

I looked him over briefly, and said, "Good to meet you, Ryan. But go ahead and just call us Jack and Logan. Coast Guard, right?"

He smiled. "Yeah. How'd you know that?"

"Your hair's too short to be a civilian, and you look too well rested to be in the Navy," I said with a laugh.

Fortunately, he didn't get offended and joined in with my laughter. "I'm guessing you're Navy, then."

"I was," I replied. "Been a civvy for almost six years now."

"No kidding. And now you're hunting pythons? What did you do in the Navy?"

"I was Special Forces."

His eyes grew wide, "Wow, like a Navy SEAL?"

"Yeah. Look, we've got the pythons over here under this tarp."

"Right," Ryan said as Jack and I led him over.

"Mitch gave me the rundown on what I'm supposed to do."

Grabbing the end of the tarp, I lifted it up and immediately wished I'd taken a video of his reaction.

"Holy shit!" he said, his jaw dropping towards the ground. "You got these this morning?"

"About thirty miles northeast of here," Jack said. "Got a honey hole for the buggers at the top of Whitewater Bay."

Ryan looked over each snake, and when he got to the big one I'd caught, he froze and shook his head. "This is unreal."

He stepped off the grass, then ran over to the back of the station and into an old wooden shed. A moment later, he appeared carrying a large object that I instantly realized was a fish scale. One of those big ones typically used to weigh marlin and tuna.

Ryan used a tape measure on the biggest one and found that it was seventeen feet, two inches long. Coiling up its massive body, we lashed it to the scale and froze in awe as the old metal needle froze at 213 pounds. As Jack had predicted, it was the largest python ever captured in the Everglades. Uncoiling its body, Jack and I gathered beside it as Martha took a few pictures.

"This will be great for spreading awareness here," she said. "Not a lot of Floridians know how bad the infestation is."

We measured and weighed the rest of the pythons, as was the protocol for hired hunters in the Everglades. When we were done, Ryan offered us seven hundred dollars for the morning's work.

"We can't accept that," I said, waving him off as he reached for a notebook to get our information to send us a check in the mail. "We do this for sport and to help protect the natural habitat here. Nothing more."

Ryan shrugged. "Are you guys sure? It's a lot of money."

I thought it over for a moment and said, "How about this? You use the money to fill up that Baia moored over there and then throw whatever's left over in that donation jar on the counter."

Smiling, Ryan said, "You got it. And thanks for your generosity."

A moment later, as we gathered the snakes into plastic bags, then hauled them into the back of Ryan's SUV, Martha turned to Ryan and said, "You don't recognize them, do you?"

"Well, you do look a little familiar," he said, looking at Jack and me. "I think I've seen your faces somewhere."

Jack and I looked at each other, confused as hell.

"I don't think we've ever met before, man," Jack said.

Martha grabbed a magazine that was rolled up in her back pocket and handed it to Ryan. His eyes darted to us, then back to the cover, and then grew real wide as the lightbulb switched on in his head. "Oh, you're the guys that found the Aztec treasure! Well, hot damn, let me at least buy you guys lunch over at the Flamingo. It's the least I could do. Horace is cooking up something fierce, as usual."

I stepped towards Ryan, looked at the cover of the *Florida Sun* magazine, then snatched it from his hands instinctively. It was a picture of Jack, Sam, myself and Nazari on the balcony of Salty Pete's, standing in front of a golden statue of Montezuma. Jack leaned over my shoulder, then gave out a long sigh.

"Well," Jack said, gathering his thoughts, "I guess it was only a matter of time before the story leaked out."

The caption under our photograph read: "Local Heroes Discover Aztec Treasure!" Opening the magazine to the story, I saw more pictures, which included a few of Neptune's Table and the salvage vessel we'd used to haul the treasure up. Under the article's title, I saw that it had been written by Harper Ridley, a journalist for the *Keynoter* out of Key West. We'd done our best to keep the whole story under wraps, utilizing Nazari's wealth and power to help us, but apparently Harper had found a way to get it out.

I smiled and shook my head. I liked Harper and always had. She'd been writing stories in the Keys since I was young, and I knew that she hadn't meant to cause any trouble. But regardless of her intention, all I could think about was the massive targets that had just been put on our backs. The fact of the matter was that Black Venom, the drug cartel we'd fought with over the Aztec treasure, was a massive organization. There was no doubt in my mind they would try to retaliate for what had happened. It was just a matter of when and how. Even with all the recent government crackdowns in Mexico, there was still a good chance that they would try and pull something off against us.

"Are you guys alright?" Ryan said. "I think it's a pretty good picture if you ask me."

I grinned, then glanced over at the Flamingo, trying to take my mind off the story. We'd been able to smell the food since we pulled into the bay, and we took Ryan up on his offer for lunch. It being too hot and humid for the patio, we ate inside and enjoyed some of the best food I'd ever had. Horace even had a special barbequed alligator. I'd never liked the taste of gator much when I was young, but Ryan had insisted, and combined with the Swamp Sauce he'd cooked it in, it actually tasted really good.

When we finished, we walked back over to the Baia and prepared to shove off. Ryan got one of the dock hands to fill up my gas tank, though it was already well over half-full, then helped me untie the mooring lines. "Say, Logan, you think you could teach me a thing or two? I'm a survival technician and part of helicopter rescue squad, just on temporary duty here before I head back to my permanent station in Key West. I'm supposed to go to self-defense school in a few months, and I'd like to show up prepared if I can."

"Sure. Small world. I've got a house there, and I keep my boat moored at the Conch Marina. Just stop by sometime and I'm sure you'll catch me. I'm at slip twenty-four."

"I'll do that. Thanks."

I jumped aboard the Baia, then turned back to Ryan. "Ryan, you mind if I have that magazine?"

"Sure, dude," he replied, pulling it from his pocket and handing it to me over the transom. "It was a pleasure to meet you. Hopefully, I'll see you again soon."

I smiled and nodded as I rolled up the magazine and slipped it into my cargo shorts pocket. Stepping into the cockpit, I started up the Baia's massive twin six-hundred-horsepower engines and eased her away from the old dock. Within a few minutes, I had her out in the open water of the Gulf, heading south.

# THREE

We cruised at a leisurely thirty knots for the first hour or so, not in any sort of hurry as we enjoyed the warm tropical wind and sunshine and sipped on a few Paradise Sunset beers. It was a special brew that had been a favorite of both of our fathers before they'd passed away. They were brewed right in Key West at Keys Disease Brewery, and although the small establishment had retired that particular brew years earlier, a little green had convinced them to bring it back. As I took a few swigs of the ice-cold liquid, I nodded and thought that it was hands down the smoothest brew I'd ever had.

As we drank and continued south along the Upper Keys, Jack and I took turns reading the article about the Aztec treasure.

"Maybe it's not such a bad thing, bro," Jack said after reading the last paragraph. He was leaning back on the white half-moon cushioned seat with the small table beside me. "I mean, it's not like Marco didn't know who we were. I'm sure he'd already relayed information to the rest of the group back in Mexico. Maybe they've just given up on their work here."

"I hope you're right," I said. But I knew that big organizations like Black Venom liked to hold a grudge. Deep down, I knew that one day they'd try and exact their revenge on us, one way or another.

"Heard anything from Scott?"

I grabbed my smartphone from my backpack on the deck beside me but saw that I'd only received one message since I'd last checked it, and it was from Sam.

"I'll give him a call later," I said. The truth was, I was just as curious as Jack was about what could be happening. I knew that being a senator and all, Scott had to deal with a lot of important issues. But having a helicopter pick him up in the middle of the Everglades? I couldn't imagine them doing that unless something serious had happened.

The message from Sam, a marine biology professor at Florida State who'd been a huge help in our discovery of the Aztec treasure, was short and sweet, just seeing how I was doing. We'd been dating for the past four months, and though she occasionally visited her home, she spent most of her time in Key West with me. I replied that everything was great and told her I'd be home in a couple of hours. I couldn't help but smile as I typed the message. It was just the effect she had on me, I guess.

After killing my first beer, I grabbed another from the large Yeti cooler behind my seat. Snatching another for Jack as well, I handed it to him and we popped the tops, then clinked the necks together and smiled as we sat back in our cushioned chairs and looked out over the beautiful blue horizon ahead of us.

"You know," Jack said while tilting his body forward and setting his bare feet on the cooler, "I've been thinking that this boat of yours really needs a name, bro."

I laughed and thought it over for a moment. The truth was, he was right. Back when I'd purchased the Baia from the previous owner, a retired surgeon who'd sold it to sail the world with his wife, he'd painted over the old name, and I'd yet to do anything except leave the hull blank. The fact was I hadn't really given it much thought, and the few ideas that had managed to wiggle their way into my mind, I'd quickly discarded as either too unoriginal or too ridiculous.

After a few moments, I shrugged and said, "Any ideas?"

As he looked out over the water, his lips contorted into a smile and he said, "Well, I was just thinking about that day we were being chased by Black Venom over by Neptune's Table. How you weaved in and out of gunfire and made it through Sierra Reef at over forty knots." Taking another sip of beer, he smiled and added, "What do you think about *Dodging Bullets*?"

I thought it over for a moment, running it over in my head and imagining it stenciled onto the dark silver hull. "*Dodging Bullets*," I said, liking the way it sounded. "I like it." Then I chuckled and added, "But you're forgetting that a few of those rounds struck the aft end of the hull. It cost me a small fortune to get them fixed."

He nodded. "Well, I didn't say you should name it *Dodging All Bullets*, did I?" He joined in with my laughter and leaned back into the chair. “I’ll call Gus and have him get a painter over to the marina as soon as possible.”

I held my beer up in the breezy air and said, “To *Dodging Bullets*.” Then Jack and I clinked our beers together and took a few long pulls.

It was just after 1400 when we reached the Lower Keys, and it was a warm, clear day out on the water. Relishing in the fresh sea air, I pushed down on the throttles and quickly brought the boat up to forty-five knots, maintaining that speed until we rounded Fleming Key and entered Man of War Harbor. Easing on the throttles, I motored us slowly past the Key West Yacht Club and into Conch Marina, passing by rows of assorted speedboats and sailboats. A lot of the slips were empty since summertime is the slow season in the Keys. This is due to the intense heat of the tropical summer, which routinely raises the mercury above the ninety-degree mark. And it’s also due to hurricanes, starting with Tropical Storm Cristobal, which made landfall in Wilmington, North Carolina, and Hurricane Dolly, which had killed one person in the Panhandle at the end of July. Fortunately, the only effect each had on the Keys was stronger winds than usual, making time out on the water difficult for a few days.

I eased the Baia into slip twenty-four, the same slip I’d used since I’d bought the boat four months earlier, and Jack tied her off. I killed the engines, then hooked up the water and shore power cables. Glancing at my phone, I saw that Sam had recently replied and told me that she’d be at the house when I got back. For the first month after finding and salvaging the Aztec treasure, Sam and I had lived together on the Baia. Then we’d found a beautiful house over on Palmetto Street, and I'd decided to become a homeowner, using the finder's fee from the portion of the treasure that was sold.

Though we'd agreed to donate most of the money, Arian Nazari, the billionaire oil tycoon who'd helped us take down Black Venom, had insisted on our accepting a four percent finder's fee, to be split amongst myself, Jack, Scott and Sam. Once all of the treasure was properly excavated and loaded carefully onto salvage vessels, we'd discovered that there were over twenty tons of gold bars that had gone down at Neptune's Table aboard the *Intrepid* almost half a century ago. Though the majority of the artifacts were given to various museums, including a handful to go on display on the second story of Salty Pete's, we'd decided to sell the gold bars. At eight hundred and sixty-nine dollars an ounce, the twenty tons equated to just over half a billion dollars. At one percent, I'd banked a cool three million, after paying Uncle Sam his dues, of course. After using a large chunk of the money to buy a house in Key West and another handful to help fix up Salty Pete's Bar and Grill, I'd stuck the rest into a savings account and hadn't touched it since.

The majority of the treasure, however, had been donated to various organizations in Mexico, many of which were run by Nazari. In just the four short months since we'd found the treasure, he'd already sent us stacks of photos showing houses, schools, libraries, wells, and other much-needed structures constructed for the poorest communities in Mexico. All in all, he estimated that over a million lives could potentially be saved by the money made from selling the treasure.

"I'm feeling a nap, and then a wild night on the

town," Jack said as he grabbed his gear and hopped over the transom. "Isaac's at a friend's house tonight, and the Wayward Suns are playing over at Pete's. What do you say, bro?"

I laughed. "The Wayward Suns? I've never heard of them."

"They're a local band from Key Largo. Sort of a Bob Marley meets the Zac Brown Band kind of sound. Just come and see them tonight." Jack grinned. "I know you'll like them, bro."

Intrigued, I told Jack that I would be there, but I had a few things I needed to get done, a couple errands and equipment I needed for the boat. And I needed to check on Sam, who I hadn't seen since the previous morning.

"The mic gets hot at nine," Jack said with a grin before throwing his gear over his shoulder and walking down the dock towards his boat.

I grabbed my black Camelbak, which held a few must-have items I took with me almost wherever I went, including my Sig Sauer P226 pistol, complete with a custom gold trident etched into the side of the slide. Bread and butter for Navy SEALs for the past twenty years, the P226 was deemed by many, including myself, to be the most reliable handgun on the planet. In my years of Navy and mercenary experience, I'd rarely gone anywhere without it strapped to my side.

The bag also had two extra fifteen-round magazines, both full at all times, my Cressi dive knife, a rain slicker, my night vision monocular, and a custom first aid kit I'd assembled based on key items I'd utilized over the years in combat situations. I'd started using the bag after having to fight off Black Venom for the Aztec treasure, knowing that I could never be too careful. If trouble ever found me, even in paradise, I'd be ready for it.

I kept my cargo shorts and tee shirt on but slipped into a pair of black low-top Converse, then locked up the Baia and headed down the dock with my backpack over my shoulder. Before I reached the mahogany stairs leading up to the parking lot, I heard a voice call out to me.

"Logan!" Turning around, I realized that it was Gus. He moved swiftly down the dock, carrying a small package in his hands. "Hey, have you talked to the sheriff yet?"

Gus Henderson was the owner of Conch Marina along with the Greasy Pelican, a restaurant that sat on pilings over the water at the edge of the marina. He'd inherited the place from his parents, to whom it had also been passed down. The Hendersons were real conchs, through and through, and were as much a part of the island as Key lime pie. He was in his early forties and about half a foot shorter than my six foot two inches. He had a strong lean build, tanned skin and curly black hair.

"Hey, Gus. The sheriff, you say?"

"Yeah," Gus said as he reached me at the base of the steps. "He came by this morning and said he needed to talk to you. Looked pretty important."

Intrigued, I asked, "He didn't say what it was about?"

Gus just shook his head, then handed me the package in his hands. "Here, this came for you today."

I smiled, knowing exactly what it was by the weight of it. My new toy had arrived. Him giving me the package reminded me that I still needed to change some of my shipping addresses to my house.

“Thanks, Gus. You going to Pete’s tonight?”

He smiled. “I wouldn’t miss a chance to see the Wayward Suns again. Those guys light it up every time.”

“See you there, then,” I said before turning and walking up the steps.

My truck, a black Toyota Tacoma four-door with an extended cab and off-road tires, was parked right up alongside a small wooden fence, facing the marina. A few months earlier, I’d been rammed off the road by Black Venom over on the Seven Mile Bridge. The Tacoma had flipped a few times and had looked like hell, but after a few weeks in the auto shop here in Key West, it looked good as new again. I slid my hand over the freshly painted exterior. Not so much as a small scratch remained from the incident.

Unlocking the door, I climbed inside, set the package and my backpack on the passenger seat beside me, started up the engine and turned onto Caroline Street. Though it wasn’t the heavy tourist season, there were a few people walking the paved sidewalks along the waterfront, watching the boats come in and out of the harbor and navigating through the gift shops and local eateries. Many restaurants closed for the summer, the owners taking a few months off to travel or unwind in preparation for another busy season in Key West. Jack owned Rubio Charters, a diving and fishing charter, and his boat, the *Calypso*, was moored just down the dock from mine in Conch Marina. Though he often talked about closing for a few months, I’d never seen him do it before. He loved the Keys and he loved taking people out on the water, watching their eyes light up as they explored all the reefs, aquatic life, and shipwrecks the islands had to offer.

It was only a five-minute drive to my house from the marina. I was just about to pull onto my street when I heard the unmistakable sounds of police sirens coming from behind me. Glancing in my rearview mirror, I saw a black-and-white Key West Police vehicle with its red and blue lights flashing behind me. Releasing the gas and easing my foot onto the brake, I pulled into the parking lot of a Fausto's Food Palace. A moment later, I saw Sheriff Wilkes climb out of the car and walk towards me, his tall, lean frame and his dark black complexion unmistakable. Though I'd been told that he was in his late forties, he still moved like a man much younger and looked more like late thirties. I rolled down my window just before he reached my door.

"You know I have a cell phone, Sheriff," I said, grinning as he placed his hand on the top of my truck and looked inside behind a pair of Oakley sunglasses. I'd only interacted with him a few times, but I'd gotten the impression that he was more of an old-school cop. The kind of guy who probably still had fax machines in his office.

"I wanted to speak with you in person, Mr. Dodge," he said. His voice was low and powerful. "Would you mind following me down to the station?"

I didn't know him very well, but I could tell that it was obviously something important. Though I was anxious to get home and check up on Sam, I knew that would have to wait.

"Sure. I'll meet you there."

"Thanks," he said as he turned and walked back to his car.

Rolling up the window and cranking up the AC, I wondered what he had to talk to me about. Whatever it was, the guy sure had a flair for the dramatic.

A few minutes later, I pulled into the parking lot in front of a two-story faded pink building with white trim and the words *Key West Police Station* over the front door. It was located right off Roosevelt Boulevard, just after where it transitioned from US-1. A moment later, Sheriff Wilkes parked right beside me and I killed the engine and stepped out. He led me into the well-air-conditioned building, past a few desks at reception and into a back office with a glass door. Ushering me inside, he offered a chair and shut the door behind us. It was the same chair I'd sat in after fighting off Black Venom at Neptune's Table four months ago. Over thirty dead guys and two yachts up in flames had made our first interaction rocky at best. The truth was that I'd never much liked dealing with law enforcement. All their regulations and traditions just seemed to make getting anything done a headache.

"I'd ask you if you know why you're here, Mr. Dodge," he said, sitting behind his desk across from me. "But that would be a waste of time. What I'm about to discuss with you is currently classified."

I nodded and rolled his words over in my mind. I was intrigued but also confused as to why, if what he wanted to discuss was classified, he'd decided to tell me. Though I still had a top-secret clearance, a status given to me while I was in the Navy and renewed a few times since, the recent events regarding Salazar were on a need-to-know basis.

When he saw that I was all ears, he continued, "How much do you know about Benito Salazar?"

I raised my eyebrows at the name. "Just basic info, really. He was captured in that raid in Miami, what? Three years ago now?"

The sheriff nodded. "Almost four. It took a while

for him to be convicted, but once he was, they locked him away for two life sentences with no chance of parole."

Benito Salazar was a notorious Cuban socialite, gambler, and murderer. He also happened to be the leader of one of Cuba's most powerful gangs, a group of outcasts who, in their heyday, had many politicians in their pockets, including a couple in the States. Salazar had been on the FBI's most wanted list for four years when he was finally captured in a shoot-out in one of his houses just outside of Miami. A few special agents had worked their way into the tight-knit group and had taken Salazar down from the inside. He'd had one of the most widely publicized trials in history. He'd tried whatever means he could, including bribes to both the judge and the lawyers, to soften the sentence handed down to him, but none of it had worked in the end.

I glanced over at the sheriff, who was eyeing me with a stone-cold expression. "What makes you bring him up?" I asked. "What? Did he finally get sick of living with himself and do the world a favor?"

He shook his head. "No, unfortunately. He escaped from El Combinado del Este Prison late last night."

My eyes grew wide quickly as he caught my full attention. El Combinado del Este was Cuba's maximum-security prison, and one of the best in the world.

"Escaped? How in the hell could he have escaped?"

"I'm not sure," he replied. "I don't have all the specifics. But I do have it on good authority that he's going to try and come to US soil."

The idea struck me as ludicrous. "Why would he

ever try something as stupid as that?" If I were the highest-profile escaped con in the world, I'd run away, get as far off the grid as possible and never stumble onto it again.

"Again, I don't know. I just wanted you to be aware of what was happening."

Antsy, I stood up from my chair and paced back and forth a few times, lost in thought. Turning to face him, I said, "You think he's gonna come here, don't you?"

He shrugged. "I just like to err on the side of caution if I can. Look, after Salazar was locked away, the gang dispersed to almost nothing. But I have no doubt that he still has followers that will remain loyal to him."

"And you're telling me all of this because…"

He grinned. "Because I've heard a lot about you, and I'm impressed by the way you handled Black Venom, even if you didn't notify us about anything." He raised an eyebrow at me, then continued, "And… because you seem to stumble into trouble a lot. I just want you to dial it down for a few weeks, until we nab this guy."

I laughed. I hadn't even been in a bar fight in four months. And technically Club Indigo wasn't even a bar. "I'll try, but I can't make any promises."

"Just call me if you learn anything, okay? I don't want to be in the dark again, like last time trouble came to Key West."

Nodding, I said, "Alright." We shook hands, and just before I turned to leave, I said, "Just out of curiosity, if this just happened, how did you hear about it so fast? No offense, but isn't this kind of thing a little above your pay grade?"

"I'm retired FBI," he replied. "Wore the suit for

twenty-six years and I still have contacts. The Keys attract a lot of people willing to sacrifice deep pockets for sandy pockets."

# FOUR

I hopped into my Tacoma and drove out of the station parking lot, heading to my house on Palmetto Street. While driving, I thought about what Sheriff Wilkes had said and about how Scott had been airlifted out of the middle of the Everglades earlier that morning. There was no doubt in my mind that Salazar escaping was the reason he had been picked up, which also meant that the threat of him coming to the States was real enough to make some waves. When I pulled into the brick driveway, driving between a row of palm trees and two pink blooming snowbushes, I saw that Sam's car, a white 2006 Ford Fiesta, was parked under the right side of the house, which was propped up on stilts.

The truth was, I hadn't really been in the market for a house. I enjoyed living on the Baia. Though it was relatively small on the inside, it was fancy, and I'd always liked the cozy feeling of sleeping on a boat. But when the stilted house on Palmetto Street had gone on the market, Jack had insisted that I tour it, assuring me that it was the perfect house for me. I guess I agreed with him, because three days after first stepping foot inside it, I was signing the papers and being handed the keys.

Driving in slowly, I parked alongside Sam's Fiesta, grabbed my backpack and the package Gus had given me, then walked for the stairs leading up the right side of the house to a wraparound porch. It was painted a light gray color with white trim, and since it was on stilts, it was designed to withstand even the strongest hurricanes and tropical storms.

Walking up the stairs, I took a quick look out back at the small covered boat lift that housed my twenty-two-foot Robalo center-console on the channel at the edge of my backyard. The great little boat had come with the house, and it was a nice way to commute to the Baia if I didn't feel like driving. Stepping towards the side door, I slid my key inside, then unlocked the door and stepped through. At only seventeen hundred square feet, the two-bedroom house felt bigger than it was, with a good-sized living room and large windows that looked out over the palm trees, green grass and the channel just beyond. It also had a nice porch that expanded off the front side and had a hammock as well as a nice barbeque. I shut the door, slid my backpack over my shoulder and set it alongside the package on the gray couch facing our television.

Hearing voices coming from the master bedroom, I walked down the small hallway.

"Sam?" I said, my voice just loud enough to be heard anywhere in the house.

"I'm in here," I heard her call out. Nudging open

the door, I saw her sitting on the edge of our king-sized bed, talking on her phone and staring at her laptop. Her dark hair was tied back, and she was wearing her sexy librarian glasses. On the other side of the room, I saw two large roller bags leaning against the wall.

She smiled as I strolled in, and I leaned in beside her and kissed her cheek. Holding her free hand against the microphone, she said, "Can you give me a minute? I just gotta finish this project."

"No worries," I replied. "I'm just gonna go for a run along the waterfront, then."

She thanked me, and as I walked out, I thought I heard a man's voice through the small phone speaker. I assumed it must have been Tony or one of her other colleagues. Changing into a pair of running shorts and a tank top, I took off down Venetian Drive and ran to the waterfront and continued along US-1. Taking the Florida Keys Overseas Heritage Trail, which spanned almost all the way from Key Largo to Key West, I headed south towards the southernmost tip of the United States.

Even though it was over eighty degrees and sunny, I didn't care. In the SEALs, I'd trained in all environments, from bone-chilling subzero snowdrifts in Alaska to scorching deserts over a hundred and twenty-degrees near California's Death Valley. Though I did get a few skeptical looks as I ran along the waterfront, enjoying the ocean breeze as I ran through Fort Zachary Taylor State Park, looped around, then headed back towards the house.

Stopping in my driveway, I placed my hands on my knees and caught my breath, which had been gone long before I'd started my finishing kick. After about a minute, I glanced at my phone and saw that I'd run nine miles at a six-minute mile pace. Not bad, though I wanted to up my speed by the time the Key West Half Marathon came around in January. Once I'd caught my breath, I did a quick thirty-minute circuit, utilizing a small gym I'd made in the space under my house by assembling a pull-up bar, punching bag, speed bag, kettlebells, battle ropes and various other equipment. By the time I was finished, my body was burning all over and it felt amazing to head upstairs, make a fruity protein shake and enjoy it on the hammock I'd installed on the porch.

Glancing down at my watch, I saw that it was just past five in the afternoon. A few clouds had rolled in, but most of the sky was a deep blue color. After I spent a few minutes enjoying the fresh air and looking out towards the end of the channel, into a narrow glimpse of open ocean beyond, the sliding glass door opened and Sam stepped out.

"How was hunting?" she said, sitting down on the white wicker chair beside me.

"Good. I got a few pictures if you want to see them," I said, handing her my phone and showing her the one of us standing next to the big python.

"Holy crap! That's enormous. You caught that?"

"Yeah, and it put up a good fight too," I said, sitting up in my hammock and placing an arm around her. Glancing towards my bedroom window, I added, "What's with the bags?"

She looked up at me from my phone, surprised by the question, then said, "Oh, I'm visiting my mom again for a few days. Leaving in the morning and should be back by next weekend."

Sam was a professor of marine geology at Florida State, and her mom lived less than an hour away from the campus on the outskirts of Wakulla

Springs. She'd been working remotely for the past four months while finishing up her research on underwater geological abnormalities near Key West. Since we'd started living together, she'd visited her mom a few times to check up on her.

"Sounds good. Hey, you don't by any chance have to work tonight, do you?"

She smiled. "What do you have in mind?"

A few hours and a hot shower later, we were out the door and climbing into my truck. The drive to Salty Pete's Bar and Grill was only about five minutes, and it being a Thursday night in the summer, the roads were mostly empty. I pulled the truck up against a railroad tie in the small gravel lot just outside Pete's restaurant, knowing full well that in less than an hour, the place would be packed. As hard as it was to believe then, Salty Pete's had been a run-down has-been of a restaurant when I'd first moved back into town four short months earlier. The roof had had missing shingles, the wooden exterior had been in dire need of a paint job, and the grounds had been covered with weeds. The inside of the restaurant had been worse, with old chairs and wobbly tables and a grungy atmosphere that led almost all of the tourists who'd managed to stumble inside off the main streets to quickly change their minds and turn around.

As we walked up the large set of stairs to the new double doors, I couldn't help but marvel at just how fast the place had changed. Pete had been extremely helpful in the discovering of the Aztec treasure, so when I'd agreed to a one percent finder's fee of the treasure, I'd given him a chunk of cash, which had allowed him to turn Salty Pete's into one of the most popular destinations in town. As soon as we opened the doors, the smell of Oz's cooking radiated into our noses and tantalized our taste buds. Smelled like fresh-grilled grouper, hogfish and, of course, spiny-tailed lobster were on the menu tonight.

The main dining area, lined with brand-new booths and tables and chairs in the middle, was almost full of people. The walls were still covered with assorted knickknacks, including the same old wooden helm, a massive fishing net decorated with crabs and shells, and pictures taken over the years around the Florida Keys. While eating lunch there a week earlier, I'd noticed that one of the pictures was of Jack's dad and my dad, taken while my dad was stationed there for a few years when I was young. Pete told me that Jack had found it in storage and thought it would be a good tribute to our late fathers. I agreed.

"Logan!" Mia said, walking towards us, balancing a big round tray filled with food on one hand and a small folding stand in her other. She had her light brown hair in a ponytail as usual and wore her green Salty Pete's tee shirt. Opening up the stand and setting the tray on top of it, she continued, "Pete's upstairs. They're testing the mics and are about to fire it up."

"That old sea devil on his best behavior?" I asked, though it was a pretty stupid question. Pete could be at church with the pope and still be the same old guy.

She smirked. "You might have to switch his beer with a Coke now and then."

I laughed and, admiring the blackened grouper sandwich and the shrimp kabobs on the plates she was handing to the group sitting in the booth beside us, I asked her to bring us a few plates upstairs. She nodded and said they'd be right up, and we headed for the wide wooden staircase.

The second story of Salty Pete's had been renovated to be partly a museum and partly an extension of the seating areas. Glass cases covered the wood floors, filled with various artifacts recovered from all over the Keys, including an entire exhibit from the *Intrepid*, the Spanish shipwreck we'd found, which had sunk carrying the Aztec treasure. The entire west wall was covered in windows and had two massive doors that were propped open with dive weights, revealing the patio. It too had been upgraded, making it big enough for a stage, ten tables and a small bar against the far side.

We stepped out into the small crowd that had already gathered and, seeing that all the tables were taken, headed for the bar. The Wayward Suns had their instruments and speakers set up and were saying "mic check" into each of their microphones. We found two stools near the end of the bar, which, like most of the furniture outside, was made of bamboo, with a white granite countertop. After ordering a couple of drinks to start off, we swiveled our padded bamboo barstools around to face the band. Jack had told me they were just getting back to the Keys after a tour around the Florida Coast. They were three guys: a lead guitarist, a bassist, and a drummer. On the bar in front of us rested a few flyers with their pictures and band information. The lead guitarist, a skinny guy with long blond dreadlocks and a dark bronze tan, had a name that sounded eerily familiar to me, though I couldn't trace it in my memory.

A newspaper slapped me on the hand as I rotated around to grab my drink. It was the *Keynoter*, and the front page had the same picture we'd seen on the cover of the magazine earlier that morning in the Everglades.

"You're famous now, scallywag!" Pete shouted, patting me on the back. Pete was in his early sixties. Thin patches of gray hair covered his tanned head, and he had a metal hook for a right hand. He was also short and had enough of a belly that I routinely urged him to ease up on the beer, advice he rarely took. He always kind of reminded me of that old captain from *The Simpsons*. "You keep navigating these waters you're treading and one day you might not be such a mainlander anymore."

"Yeah right!" Jack said, appearing from behind me. He was wearing a cutoff shirt, board shorts, and flip-flops. "Logan here may not have been born in the Keys, but he's as much of a conch as anyone in the islands." Turning to the bartender, he said, "Can I get a Corona with lime?"

"Being a conch is a birthright," Pete growled, "but I guess there can be an exception made." Turning to Sam, who was sitting quietly beside me, he added, "It's good to see you out, Sam. I was beginning to think you'd never leave that house."

"Thanks, Pete," she said with a friendly smile. "It's good to see you too. I've just been really caught up in my work lately."

"Well, sit back and relax tonight, then. And I'm glad it isn't me. I was beginning to think my hook here was scaring you away." He raised it in the air. "Did I ever tell you how I lost it?"

She laughed. "Sharks while diving Goblin's Gull."

"Great white sharks," he added. "The biggest ones that ever lived."

As they continued, I turned to Jack. "Seems

busier around town than usual."

He nodded. "A cruise ship just pulled in a few hours ago. Must be trying to escape the coming storm. I've never understood why cruise lines bother during cane season. Just seems damn foolish to me."

"Coming storm?" I asked, raising my eyebrows.

"Yeah. Tropical Storm Fay is swirling just south of the DR. She's building up strength. And pretty quickly at that."

"She heading for Key West?"

He shrugged. "Not projected to, but these big storms have minds of their own."

Mia arrived a few minutes later with two plates of food and set them on the bar in front of Sam and me. Blackened grouper sandwiches with specialty sweet potato fries and a shrimp kabob over pineapple slices. I took a bite and savored the flavor as Pete walked up to the stage and introduced the band. Within seconds, they were rocking the neighborhood, belting out originals about island living in a cross between Reggae and country music, just as Jack had said. They were one of the first new bands I'd liked in a while, a band you could dance to but also listen to while just sitting on a beach chair, staring off at the ocean. Off in the distance, the sun was just starting to set over the horizon. From the patio, there was an almost completely unobstructed 180-degree view of the ocean.

A few hours later, after we'd finished our food and downed our share of drinks, Sam asked if we could leave. Glancing at my watch, I saw that it was nearing 2200, the time the band was scheduled to play until. Reaching into my wallet, I grabbed a crisp hundred-dollar bill and set it beneath my empty glass on the bar. I'd fought with Mia enough times about her not wanting me to pay that I'd learned to just leave cash and go.

As I followed Sam to the doors, my eyes were drawn to the table closest to the stage, where four rough-looking biker dudes sat drunk out of their minds. During breaks in the music, they'd heckled the band a few times. It had started off innocent at first but gradually gotten more profane as the night and their intoxication had progressed. It had caught my eye a few times, but as we moved towards the door, they were yelling over the music, and I could tell that they were getting on the band's nerves.

"Hold on a minute," I said to Sam, who had just stepped through the double doors. She shot me a confused look, then bit her lip.

Walking back out towards me, she said, "What is it?"

"I don't like this," I said, staring at the four guys sitting near the stage. I had asked Pete about them, and he'd said he'd never seen them before. They were mainlanders, drifters probably, just passing through on their motorcycles and obviously looking for trouble.

Suddenly, one of the guys threw a beer can at the lead singer, Cole Daniels, causing him and the other two guys to stop playing.

"I'm sorry, folks," Cole said. "We would love to keep entertaining you tonight, but if these guys in the front don't cool it, we're out of here. And I'm sure Sheriff Wilkes would love to come down here and kick you boys out. So, what's it gonna be? You gonna let us play or what?"

The crowd cheered and clapped, but one of the guys in front yelled something back. I couldn't hear it over the crowd, but when the noise died down, I heard the end of it.

"And if you call your sheriff," one of the biker guys said, "we'll kick his ass too." Mia was walking by their table. She had an uncomfortable look on her face, and before she could pass by, the guy continued, "Ain't that right, pretty lady?" Then he slapped her butt loud enough for me to hear it easily by the doors.

That was my cue. It got all of my blood boiling in an instant, and I weaved effortlessly in and out of people, chairs, and tables, heading for the seated bikers.

# FIVE

I calmed my breathing as I planned out an attack. They were big guys, all four of them, and I figured, judging from my vantage point at the other end of the patio, they were all in their thirties or forties. But before I reached their table to confront them, I realized that I'd been beaten to the punch.

The drummer, Blake, whose name I had seen on the poster, had stood up. He looked to be about six and a half feet tall and probably tipped the scale at over three hundred pounds. He stepped down from the stage, stood in front of the bikers' table, pointed a finger at them and told them to leave. All that did was rile them up, though, and in the blink of an eye, the guy sitting closest to Blake stood and slugged him square in the nose without a word.

Blood gushed out as Blake took a step back. He held a hand up to his face, trying to slow the blood, which was quickly soaking the top of his white undershirt.

“Sit your ass back down and play, drummer boy!” the guy barked.

Before Blake could reply, I moved between the bikers’ table and the stage. I eyed the four guys intensely, and before I spoke one of the guys took a long, hard pull from his beer, then slammed the bottle into the table, shattering the glass.

“Hey, down in front, jackass!” the guy barked. He wore a leather vest and a black headband and had long frizzled hair and a gross handlebar mustache. He eyed me angrily when I didn’t even flinch at his words.

“You guys have two choices,” I said loud enough for the entire crowd to hear me. “You either apologize to this woman and apologize to the band for all your heckling, sit your butts down and be respectful for the rest of the night, or we’ll call an ambulance and have all four of you carried out of here. What’s it gonna be, jackass?”

The guy with the headband, who I quickly realized was their leader, smirked at me and told me to get lost. He quickly pushed his chair back and rose to his feet. He was a little shorter than my six foot two, but he easily had fifty pounds on me, though I was sure it was mostly excess weight.

Before he could finish taking one step in my direction, I shifted my weight to my left leg, leaned sideways and snapped my right leg, slamming my heel into the guy’s jaw. It was a powerful side kick that knocked the guy off his feet, launching him backward. His body crashed onto the table, breaking glasses and knocking plates of food to the floor. The table wobbled a few times, then collapsed under the guy’s weight, leaving him unconscious and covered in a pile of broken dishes and food.

The three other guys knocked their chairs back and jumped to their feet. The youngest of the group, a ripped guy with slicked-back black hair, grabbed a beer bottle and shattered the end of it on a chair. He lunged at me from my right side, then stabbed the jagged end of the bottle through the air towards my face. Stepping to the side, I kicked his shin while simultaneously wrapping my arm around his back. Using his momentum against him, I hinged his body down and slammed his head into the corner of the stage. What remained of the bottle smashed to the floor, and his body went limp.

Turning around, I was barely able to deflect a punch from a guy who looked like a Viking. He had long blond hair, deep blue eyes, an aquiline nose and a massive frame. His fist, which had been aiming for the middle of my chest, only grazed my left shoulder, but it still hurt like hell. Focusing on his fist, I realized that he was gripping a shiny set of brass knuckles, making any landed punch do twice as much damage as ordinary bone.

The last guy appeared out of nowhere, carrying a wooden chair over his head. He was shorter than the other guys, stocky, and he had a bald head and a large silver earring. He seemed even more intoxicated than the others, so as he swung the chair at me, I used it against them, ducking out of the way at the last second, allowing it to slam into Blondie's back. The chair broke into pieces as Blondie yelled out in pain, then cursed out his buddy.

Kneeling down, I snatched two of the broken chair legs, reared them back, then slammed them against Blondie's ears, sandwiching his head between the lacquered bamboo. He fell to the floor and pressed his hands up to his damaged ears while blood started to flow out. He screamed in agony, and I could tell that I'd probably punctured both of his eardrums.

Baldy, having seen that he was the last of his buddies still on his feet, glanced over at me, then reached for something on his waist. Tightening my grip on the chair leg in my right hand, I threw a fastball right into his forehead, causing his body to jerk backward. The revolver he'd been reaching for rattled to the floor as I charged him. In an instant, I slammed his head into the floor, then punched him twice in the face. As I climbed off him, he was struggling to breathe and spitting out blood and saliva.

The ordeal had felt like it lasted an eternity, but I knew that it had only been a couple of seconds. My heart rate and my adrenaline had slowed things down, but as I stood and assessed the damage, it started to wear off.

"Mia, call the police," I said, glancing at her behind the bar counter. "And have them send an ambulance."

"Already done, Logan," she replied, staring at me and the four beat-up troublemakers at my feet. "They're on their way."

I nodded and, stepping over slicked-back hair guy, I grabbed the revolver from the floor. A moment later, Pete appeared carrying a bag of large plastic zip ties, which we used to secure all four of the guys' hands behind their backs. Not that it mattered much—two of them were unconscious, and the other two weren't going anywhere under their own strength anytime soon. As myself, Pete and a few other guys who were on the patio moved the bikers off to the corner, Jack walked out casually from inside the restaurant.

"Jeez, man," he said, his eyes growing wide as he saw the four guys. "I go to the can for two minutes and I miss all the fun."

Within a few minutes, the sound of police sirens filled the evening air. Red and blue lights flickered from the front of the restaurant as police cars and two ambulances arrived in the parking lot. Soon they were up on the patio, checking the guys' vital signs and strapping them to stretchers. Sheriff Wilkes was there, along with a few other officers I'd never met before. As the four guys were being carried out by the paramedics on stretchers, the sheriff looked over at me, shaking his head.

"Is this your idea of lying low?" he said. "We just talked about this today, Logan."

"These guys punched the drummer in the face," I said, not bothering to hide my frustration. "And they were harassing Mia. They were all overdrinking, yelling at people, threatening and cussing them out."

Still aggravated, he said, "You really kicked the crap out of a few of these guys." He motioned to the short bald guy whose face was covered in blood. "Was it all necessary? You don't think you were at all excessive?"

"They came at me with broken bottles, brass knuckles, and a revolver. They were trying to kill me, and they would have without hesitation if given the chance. You can't show mercy to guys like that because that's how you end up dead."

"It's all true," Pete said, stepping in and vouching for me. "Everyone here saw it. Logan here saved us all from an unfortunate and dangerous situation."

Blake the drummer stepped over to us at the edge of the stage. He was holding an ice pack up to his nose. Patting me on the back, he thanked me for stepping in. "What kind of martial arts was that anyway?" he asked.

"It's a combination of a lot of styles I've picked up over the years," I told him, then turned back to the sheriff. "Look, I only did what anyone with my training should do. As far as statements go, I'm sure you'll want one, and I'll be happy to give it." I lied, of course, about being happy to do it. I hated dealing with authorities, and I hated giving statements.

Before the sheriff could reply, Cole, the lead guitarist, grabbed the microphone and said, "Let's give a round of applause for Logan Dodge, ladies and gentlemen," he said, his voice booming over the speakers. "This last song is for you, brother."

The three members of the band gathered onstage, fired up their instruments and played one final song, ending the evening on a good note.

"Obviously you were in the right here," Sheriff Wilkes finally said. "I apologize. But I still need you to stop by the station tomorrow."

I nodded at him and told him I'd be there. I walked back over to the bar, a few people patting me on the back as I sat on a barstool. Looking across the patio, I saw Sam walking over to me.

"Are you okay?" she asked, looking me over from head to toe.

"My hands are a little the worse for wear," I replied, looking at my beat-up knuckles. "And my shoulder's bruised a little, but other than that, not a scratch."

She grabbed my hands, examined them and shook her head. "Let's get you home and take care of this."

A few guys offered to buy me a beer, but I had to

respectfully decline. After their final song, Sam and I walked through the double doors, headed down the stairs and out the front door. Parked just outside were four classic Harleys being loaded up onto a tow truck. I smiled as I climbed into my Tacoma, started up the engine and drove us back to the house.

# SIX

"You haven't said two words since we left Pete's place," I said, glancing at Sam, who was sitting on the couch, typing something on her laptop. "Is everything okay?"

I thought about her mom and how she'd been sick lately. I knew that it was hard for Sam to be away from her so much. Grabbing an ice pack from the freezer, I pressed it against my left shoulder. After sliding out of my tee shirt and examining the wound, I'd found a dark blackish-purple bruise leaving the imprint of the brass knuckles on my skin from where Blondie had hit me. Sam stopped typing and looked up at me as I filled a US Navy glass with ice water and took a few swigs. Though we'd only been together for a few months, I'd felt like I knew her pretty well, and she was the type of person who, when having trouble, liked to lose herself in her work.

"I'm fine. I just really need to get this done."

She went back to typing, and I moved to the

other side of the room, opened the sliding glass door and breathed in the fresh Caribbean air. I loved living so close to the ocean, with its crashing waves, soaring birds, and spectacular sunsets.

"Something you need to get done before your visit tomorrow?" I said, moving over to her. "Maybe I can help."

She stopped typing, sighed and drew her gaze to meet mine.

"I'm not visiting, Logan," she said. "I'm moving back."

"Moving back?" I said, unable to stop my mouth from dropping open. "Why?"

She took in a deep breath and shut her laptop. "Because it's my home. I have a career there and… I have family there."

"I've told you before that your mom is welcome here if you need to take care of her. A woman like you would have no trouble getting work here if you really wanted. Hell, you remember meeting the owner of the Dolphin Research Center in the Middle Keys? That guy practically offered you a job right there on the spot. Plus, with the reward money we got, you—"

"Don't say it." She raised her hand, stopping me. "I love my work and you know that. And it's not just my mom."

The words cut deep. Somehow, I knew what she was trying to tell me. I guess I just didn't want to believe it. I hadn't had feelings like the ones I had for Sam in a long time, maybe ever, and I didn't want to imagine that it could be over, or maybe that it hadn't ever been as good as I'd thought it was. But as she sat in front of me, saying it, it all made sense.

"I'm engaged, Logan."

The words hurt much more than I thought they

would. I got a tight, tingling feeling in my gut, and my head was in disarray. The idea that, after the past four months we'd spent together, she'd been engaged the whole time, was tough to take in.

She shook her head and looked down at the floor. "We'd been taking a break. Cold feet. Whatever. But we've been talking, and we want to go through with the marriage. We've been together almost ten years, Logan."

I really didn't care to hear any more. It was clear that she didn't want to be with me, and I only wished that she'd made up her mind sooner. The weight of her words hit me, and I dropped down into the recliner, set my glass on the coffee table and stared up at the ceiling.

She stood and placed a hand on my shoulder. "I'm sorry, Logan." She took in a deep breath and let it out, having a hard time finding the right words to say. "Look, I really loved…" But her words trailed off in my mind, and I didn't hear a thing after that. I didn't need words. I needed to be away from her.

Walking for the door, I threw my ice pack into the sink, grabbed my wallet and keys from the glass dish by the rain slicker rack, and opened the front door. Sam walked towards me and tried to say something, but I cut her off.

"Shut the door on your way out," I said, my voice lifeless and stern. Thumping down the stairs, I opened my truck, jumped inside and started the engine. After taking a few deep breaths and realizing that Sam wasn't coming after me, I backed out of the driveway and pulled onto Palmetto Street.

The next morning, I woke up unable to feel anything except throbbing pain radiating from deep within my skull. Bright light blinded my eyes as I tried to open them, trying to figure out where in the hell I was. I was lying on my back on a hard wooden surface, and as the blurry room around me came into focus, I realized I was in a bar.

I rolled onto my side and had a strong desire to find a glass of water. My mouth was as dry as a desert, and my stomach churned like it was trying to fight me. As I cleared the cloud of haze from my brain, I realized that I was at Pete's, on the first floor, lying on the bar with empty bottles of Captain Morgan and Jack Daniels all around me and blinding sunlight blazing in between the curtains.

"What in the hell did you do to yourself last night, Logan?" I said to myself as I tried my best to sit up. Then I remembered Sam and bits and pieces of the conversation we'd had.

"Funny, I was just about to ask the same thing," I heard a voice say from across the room. Looking in the direction of the sound, I saw Pete standing in the doorway, holding a cleaning rag.

Glancing around at the empty bottles, I sighed and said, "I'm sorry about the mess. And I'll pay for the alcohol." I reached for my wallet, but it wasn't in my pocket where I thought I'd left it.

Pete stepped towards me and waved me off. "Forget about it, mate. This place would still be a run-down shanty and I'd be struggling just to pay the bills if it wasn't for you."

"Thanks," I said while heaving myself off the counter and balancing on the floor as best as I could.

"I'm curious, though, what made you come back here?"

"I didn't want to be home, and my boat doesn't have enough liquor aboard."

Pete walked over and set a glass on the counter

beside me. It was full of a green and orange liquid and it looked disgusting. I gagged a little just looking at it.

"What is that?"

"Best remedy for a hangover," he said, sliding it closer to me. "And by the looks of things, you drank more than I sell sometimes in an entire evening. Just down it nice and fast and you won't taste it too much."

I was skeptical but willing to do anything to get rid of my headache. Grabbing the glass, I brought it up to my mouth and chugged all of it in a few seconds. Wiping my mouth with the back of my hand, I set the empty glass back on the counter. It tasted like tomato, carrot and cucumber juice.

"How in the hell did you get past the security system anyway?" Pete asked after I'd let the drink sit in my stomach for a moment.

"I installed the security system," I reminded him. "And you gave me a key anyway, remember?"

He smiled, and as he nodded, I walked for the door. "Thanks for the drink, but I gotta go."

"You know," Pete said, raising his voice so I could hear him, "things like this happen sometimes. I've owned this restaurant for thirty years. You see a lot of things in that time. But seeing you in here really surprised me. I never thought you to be the type." I stopped for a moment, then opened the front door. "How are you and Sam doing? She seemed a little distant last night."

I took in a deep breath, then let it all out and said, "She left."

Shutting the door, I labored into my truck and headed back to my house. Part of me hoped I'd still see her white Fiesta in the driveway, that maybe she'd come to her senses and changed her mind, deciding to stay here with me in Key West. Another part of me hoped she wouldn't be there, not wanting to ever see her face again. Driving into the parking lot, I saw that the space beneath my house was empty of cars. I parked my truck and headed inside to gather some supplies.

Most everything I needed was already on the Baia, but I also wanted to check up on the house and make sure it was all locked up. The front door was unlocked, and she'd left the porch light on. Moving into the master bedroom, I opened my safe and grabbed my .338 Lapua sniper rifle, which had a Nightforce NXS scope attached to it. Then, after locking it back up, I threw a sleeping bag, sleeping pad, and my Exped Mira two-person tent into a sack. In the pantry, I grabbed a few MREs, two extra waterproof lighters, and three small propane tanks for the portable stove I kept on the boat. Loading everything over my shoulder and carrying my rifle in my hand, I grabbed the package Gus had given me, then turned out the lights, locked up the house and loaded everything into the bed of my Tacoma.

I started up the engine and backed out of the driveway. Cruising onto Roosevelt Boulevard and over the Palm Avenue Causeway, I rolled down the windows, allowing the fresh morning breeze to blow through my hair as I cracked open a Sunset Paradise beer and took a few long pulls. Though it was barely ten, the day was already hot and the sky bright as hell, forcing me to wear a pair of black-rimmed Oakleys I kept in the center console. Pulling into the parking lot of the Conch Marina, I parked the truck, grabbed my gear and headed down the mahogany steps to the dock. It was pretty quiet, which was typical for a

Friday morning, and as I walked, I only saw a few people hanging out on their boats.

When I reached the Baia at slip twenty-four, I stepped over the transom and set all my gear on the half-moon table. Stepping down into the galley, I grabbed a bag of extra shorts and tee shirts, along with a towel, and set them beside the rest of my gear. Then I grabbed all of my spearfishing and lobster diving gear, including my mask, free diving fins, and snorkel. I also grabbed the package Gus had given me the previous day. Cutting into it with my dive knife, I pulled out a brand-new top-of-the-line spear gun that had thick rubber bands with over eighty pounds of draw strength. After looking it over for a moment, I set it on the table along with three metal spears and my old spear gun that I'd used for the past few months.

Tied off onto the port side of the Baia was my fifteen-foot red Zodiac, which had a seventy-horsepower Yamaha engine clamped onto its stern. Handful by handful, I loaded all my gear onto the inflatable boat, including my Subgear Prolight flashlight, a Condor machete, a compass, an insect-repellent device, a portable stove with a canister of extra propane, a cooler, a five-gallon plastic container of freshwater and my black Camelbak with some of my necessities inside it. I only took enough to live comfortably for a couple of days, not wanting to weigh my Zodiac down too much. I had a good distance to travel and didn't want it to take all day.

Reminding myself that it had been over ten years since I'd gone where I was planning to go, I stepped back down into the salon and grabbed my dad's old map of the Lower Keys. Looking northwest of Dry Tortugas National Park, I spotted a blotch of blue ink my dad had used to mark an island.

My head was still spinning, partly from the disgusting amount of alcohol and partly because I couldn't get Sam's face out of my mind. I guess everyone handles bad news differently, and I'd do what I usually did. I'd get away from the world for a few days, maybe more, and just keep to myself as I wrapped my head around what had happened. The day I'd found out my dad had died, I had taken my old sailboat out to Catalina Island, a tropical paradise twenty miles west of Los Angeles, and spent two weeks moored in one of the less popular areas of the island. I'd spent my afternoons freediving, spearfishing, hiking and thinking about all the times my dad and I had spent together. And that was what I had to do now, I said to myself as I grabbed another beer from my fridge for the road, still unable to comprehend what had happened the night before.

"Logan," a voice said. It came from the dock, and as I looked through the haze of my vision, I saw Jack standing just aft of the stern. We made eye contact for a second, then I locked up the Baia and shuffled over to the port side. Jack sighed. "Pete told me what happened. Are you gonna be okay, bro?"

I stepped over the side and landed on my Zodiac. Turning around, I reached for the line tied to the Baia.

"Look, you're my friend and I hate to say this, but it's true," he said, stepping to the edge of the dock. "These things happen all the time down here. Women get swept off their feet, caught up in the beauty of the islands, the crystal-clear water, the warm blue sky and the laid-back lifestyle. Then, eventually, they realize they have to go back to where they came from. I'm sorry, bro." He glanced away, shaking his head. "Damn, and I really liked her too."

There was a brief silence as I coiled up the rope, then scooted onto the cushioned bench seat just aft of the helm. Jack examined all of my gear and said, "Where are you going?"

"Look, I need to get away," I snapped. "I need to be alone for a little while."

"Damn, Logan you can't go out in this little skiff with a tropical storm barreling this way." He sighed, then continued, "It's turned north, and its seventy miles per hour winds are pummeling through the DR as we speak, and there are predictions it'll head this way. If it does, you're looking at probably no more than a couple of days until it makes landfall. I know you're well-traveled, but I've experienced hundreds of Florida storms in my life. You don't want to mess with them, Logan. Especially a big one like Fay."

I took in a deep breath, then let it out. Jack was right. It was a stupid thing to do, but I had to leave. Just the way I was. "I'll only be gone a few days," I said. "If Fay swirls near, then I'll head back. This isn't my first storm either, man."

In an instant, Jack leapt over the transom and stormed down into the salon. A moment later, he reappeared carrying my portable satellite phone.

"Here," he said, tossing it to me. I caught it with one hand. "Because I'm sure your stubborn butt didn't grab one."

# SEVEN

I stowed the satellite phone in the small compartment next to the helm, then inserted the key and started up the Yamaha. Then, grabbing my Keys Disease beer and taking two more swigs, I wiped the foam from my lips and eased the Zodiac out of the marina. Cruising out between Fleming Key and Wisteria Island, I punched the throttles, sending the inflatable boat cruising through the ocean at over thirty knots.

There were a few other boats out on the water, but as I cruised past the Marquesas Keys, I had most of the horizon to myself in all directions. It's sixty-seven miles from Key West to Dry Tortugas National Park, and after a little over two hours of cruising west, I passed the red brick walls of Fort Jefferson. Rising forty-two feet above the water below, the old fort's walls form a hexagon that encloses sixteen acres, surrounding most of the island. On the southern end of the island, there was a small pier with a white ferry moored against it, shuttling tourists back and forth between there and Key West.

As I cruised beyond Fort Jefferson, I passed by Brilliant Shoal, White Shoal, and Loggerhead Key, with its old white-and-black-striped lighthouse in the distance. Then it was mostly open ocean for another fifteen miles until I saw my destination, the island of Monte Cristo, peeking over the horizon. Monte Cristo was only about two acres at high tide, but unlike most every other island off the southern tip of Florida, it had pretty good elevation. The highest point, a jutting cliff rising into the tropical air, was about sixty feet above sea level. The cliffs provided sufficient cover from tropical winds but had turned off most everyone from exploring it. From a distance, the island looked like nothing more than a useless pile of rocks, and nothing like any other island I'd seen in the Keys.

Fortunately, my dad had explored it and had found a narrow channel between the cliffs that led to a cove and a small sandy beach. The island was also surrounded by a shallow reef, making it accessible only by boats with less than a few feet of draft, even at high tide. This was the main reason I'd decided on the Zodiac instead of the Baia. If I'd brought the Baia, I would've had to anchor her almost a quarter of a mile from the island.

I eased off the throttles as I cruised over the shallow reefs, peeking over the pontoons and admiring the colorful sea life below. The reefs were littered with sea urchins, starfish, conch shells, hermit crabs, jellyfish, and an abundance of tropical fish. I spotted more than one set of antennas sticking out from crevices in the reef below, making my stomach grumble as my body anxiously anticipated a feast of fresh lobster.

It was just after two in the afternoon when I

reached the island. The sky was full of nothing but blue and the water was calm, allowing me to navigate to the northwest side of the island easily. When I reached the location where the cliffs opened up, I cruised down to only a few knots and turned sharply to port. The narrow channel between the cliffs was less than ten feet wide, making it difficult to navigate through and almost impossible to spot from a distance.

I eased the Zodiac around a corner, then entered a beautiful tropical oasis. A lagoon that covered less than half an acre of perfectly calm crystal-clear water and a white sandy beach about thirty feet wide. Punching the throttles, I rocketed the Zodiac onto the beach, sliding up over the sand.

I spent the next hour or so setting up my camp, choosing a flat surface near the middle of the island between two large palm trees that offered an incredible view of the Gulf of Mexico on one side and the Caribbean Sea on the other. Once my tent was set up, my gear stowed, and the Zodiac brought up and tied off, I grabbed my dive bag and my new spear gun. Strapping my Cressi dive knife to my leg, I slipped out of my shirt and sandals, donned my mask and snorkel, and waded out into the water, carrying my fins in one hand and my bag and spear gun in the other. Once I was waist-deep, I donned my fins and slipped my mask up over my face. Strapping my bag to a dive belt around my waist, I grabbed hold of the spear gun with both hands and dropped down into the warm water.

An underwater world of vibrant color revealed itself behind the curtain of the surface. The clear water of the lagoon was teeming with life, creatures escaping the harsh open ocean and thriving in their own private paradise. The lagoon was about twenty feet deep at its center, and though it was full of lobster, crabs, and fish, my dad and I had always preferred to go for the ones outside the channel, leaving the ones inside alive, just in case we ever had no luck in the open ocean.

With one breath, I finned to the bottom and skirted through the channel, my spear gun aiming ahead of me. Searching the reefs that surrounded the island, I bagged four bugs that were all well above regulation size and speared a large red grouper along with a yellowtail snapper. On my way back to the lagoon, I passed by a large green sea turtle feasting on a deep blue moon jellyfish. I also swam by two lemon sharks that eyed the fish in my left hand for a moment before scurrying off into the distance.

When I had reached my private beach, I slipped out of my fins and carried my spoils up to my camp just a few hundred feet from the water. The name Monte Cristo had been my idea, and since the island had no official name, it was what myself, my father and Jack referred to it by. *The Count of Monte Cristo* had always been one of my favorite adventure stories as a kid, and at a young age, I'd recognized the similarities between the island in the story and this little island northwest of Dry Tortugas. Both appeared rocky and uninhabitable from afar, and both hid secrets from the outside world. Though our Monte Cristo didn't have any hidden gold on it, at least not that we were aware of, the hidden paradise behind the cliffs had been treasure enough for us.

After an hour or so, I had my fish and lobster tails cleaned, seasoned with Swamp Sauce and cooked using my portable propane grill. Using a native climbing method, I scaled one of the coconut trees beside my tent, freed four coconuts and cut into them using my machete. As the sun started to fall into the ocean over the western horizon, I laid out a few portions of food on a plastic tray and carried it over to the hammock I'd set up between two palm trees right by the cliffside.

Lying in the hammock, I savored the fresh seafood, enjoying every tantalizing bite and washing it all down with fresh coconut juice, straight out of the coconut. I'd set up a portable mosquito-repelling device, one that I'd first used in South America, and it along with the ocean breeze made the tropical air free of bugs.

After finishing my meal, I watched the sun as it turned the sky dark red, with tints of brilliant oranges and yellows. As it fell, I thought about Sam and all the amazing times we'd spent together over the past few months. It hurt to think that maybe I had never been anything more than a distraction for her, that maybe she'd never had the same feelings for me that I'd had for her. I'd never been the type of guy to have serious relationships, but after spending the last four months with her, I'd felt something more. Something I hadn't felt for a woman in a very long time.

"Maybe some guys just aren't cut out for marriage," I said to myself as I finished off another coconut and watched as the last hint of the dying sun sank into the sea.

Falling asleep on the hammock, I woke up and spent the next day intermittently swimming around the island and lounging in the hammock, trying to get over Sam. The sky had been clear all day and the air warm. The silence of the island helped me recharge and feel in tune with myself and with nature. It was what I'd always loved about camping. Just the silence and the peacefulness of it all. When I woke up the second morning, however, that peacefulness was gone, replaced by something much less friendly.

# EIGHT

I practically fell out of my hammock as I was awoken by the sound of thunder roaring far off in the distance. Balancing on my bare feet and shaking the sleepiness from my body, I looked around and felt a stiff breeze whip past me, shaking the palm leaves softly overhead and swaying the trunks. My head spun, and I remembered that I'd downed an entire bottle of Silver Patrón the night before, leaving me with one hell of a hangover.

"Crap," I said to myself as I ran over to the cliff for a better view of the sky and the ocean.

Though the sun had yet to make its appearance, it lit up the sky enough for me to see the massive swirl of black clouds that had rolled in and the whitecaps that had formed over the water. Taking it all in, there was no doubt in my mind that, as Jack had predicted might happen, Tropical Storm Fay had changed course and was now about to make landfall in the Keys.

Glancing at my dive watch, I saw that it was almost 0500. I'm usually a pretty light sleeper, but I guess I had the alcohol to blame. I knew that I would have to get my butt out of there in a hurry if I was going to escape the brunt of the storm. Jack had told me that Fay had had winds in excess of seventy miles per hour when she'd rammed through the DR. I wouldn't be able to withstand such a force on Monte Cristo, and especially not in a tent. I had to get off the island and back to Key West, and I had to do it fast.

In less than fifteen minutes, I had everything packed up and stowed securely on my Zodiac. Even in that short amount of time, the winds had picked up strength noticeably, and even my private lagoon had small whitecaps when I untied the rope and shoved off. Starting up the engine, I turned around and carefully cruised through the narrow channel. When I reached the end of it, the bow of the Zodiac rose four feet into the air, then splashed down as a wave passed by. It was still pretty dark, but I could see well enough to maneuver myself around the island and head back towards Key West using my compass.

The waves rocked my small boat as I picked up speed, splashing foamy water over the inflatable pontoons and into my face. Thunder roared again from behind me, only this time it was louder. The storm was quickly barreling towards me, and all I could do was try and escape it in time.

After thirty minutes of crashing through waves that were growing larger with each passing second, I saw a white light flickering in the distance off my starboard side. I wiped the saltwater from my eyes, focused on the light and realized that it must have been the Dry Tortuga Lighthouse on Loggerhead Key. A massive wave slammed into me from behind, surging the stern up and then slamming it down in a massive and chaotic splash. Water covered my feet and soaked my clothes. I knew that my Zodiac would soon capsize if the waves continued to get bigger at their current rate.

I took a moment to think through my situation. Judging by the winds, the waves, and the black clouds looming overhead, I wouldn't make it to Key West in time. Even if I pushed my Zodiac to its limits, it would take hours, provided I never capsized along the way. I decided that my only option was to head for Fort Jefferson and wait out the storm within its walls. I had enough provisions to survive, so long as I could stay sheltered from the storm.

I altered my course slightly, cruising towards the lighthouse, where I would then wrap around the northern tip of Loggerhead Key and cruise straight for Fort Jefferson. I cursed myself for being so stupid, so reckless, and for failing to heed the warnings I'd been given. I wasn't usually the guy who went into things unprepared, and yet there I was, trying to outrun a tropical storm in a fifteen-foot Zodiac. My anger and frustration had clouded my reason, and I would have to pay for it the hard way.

As I made my way towards the northern end of Loggerhead Key, cruising as fast as I could through the roaring waves, something caught my eye on the shore. Every time the light from the lighthouse flickered, I saw a brilliant dark-blue-and-white object stuck in the sand between the crashing waves and the shrub line. At about half a mile away, it was impossible to see exactly what it was, but I knew that it must have been a boat of some kind. As I reached within five hundred feet of the shore, I realized that it was a large yacht and that its dark blue hull appeared to be cracked and riddled with bullet holes. The aft section was jerking up and down with each violent, crashing wave.

Someone was having a pretty bad day, I thought as I cruised closer to the wreck to get a better look, wondering what in the hell had happened. The sun was starting to rise, allowing me to see some details of the boat through the heavy rain and winds. There was nobody in sight, but when I'd cruised to just a few hundred feet from the crashing waves, I heard the unmistakable sound of a gunshot echoing from the center of the island. If it had been a normal day, I would have killed the engine and listened intently for the source of the sound. But with the rain howling against me, the waves splashing over the pontoons of my Zodiac, and the thunder roaring, I had no way to tell where exactly the weapon had been fired from. All I knew was that it had come from inland, near the lighthouse.

The sound of a second gunshot cracked through the air, and I knew that someone must be in trouble. Looking ahead, I saw the old brick walls of Fort Jefferson looming in the shadowy distance, just three miles from Loggerhead Key. Looking over in the direction where gunshots had come from, I knew that I had to figure out what was happening and see if I could help. Instinctively, I grabbed my Sig and leg holster out of my backpack and strapped it to my right thigh along with an extra magazine.

Following an unusually large wave, I turned the helm sharply to the right, putting me on a direct course for the beach. Easing forward on the throttles, I picked up speed, then killed the engine and raised the propeller from the water just as the Zodiac's hull hit the beach. The fiberglass hull scraped over the fine white sand, slowing the boat to an abrupt stop. I grabbed the nylon rope and leapt over the bow, landing in wet sand that oozed up over my ankles.

Wrapping an arm inside the boat and grabbing hold of a handle, I dragged the Zodiac all the way up past the shrub line and quickly tied the rope off around a thick branch of what looked like a large wax myrtle plant. Reaching for my Sig, I unholstered it and held it firmly with both hands as I headed over towards the yacht. She was a beauty, a fifty-two-foot Regal yacht that must have set the owner back at least a million bucks. There were at least thirty bullet holes riddled all over its hull, and it had massive cracks near the forward section, where portions of the hull had been smooshed in like an accordion. Clearly, the pilot had hit a few of the shallow reefs nearby before he'd crash-landed on the shores of Loggerhead.

Splashing through the crashing waves, I jumped, grabbed hold of the railing and pulled myself up onto the deck. The hatch leading down into the salon and cabins was open and slamming violently back and forth on its hinges, a sign that whoever had been there had left, and probably in a hurry.

I did a quick search of the boat, though much of it was flooded, then ran and jumped back onto the beach. Running up the sand, I did a quick sweep of the area and realized that, less than a quarter of a mile down the beach, another boat was tied off. From where I was, it looked like one of those rugged patrol boats designed for taking on rough seas. I'd always referred to that style of boat as a storm chaser, since its aluminum hull rose all the way up and over the cockpit and was built strong, able to withstand even the worst storms. It had a partially enclosed cockpit and a pair of what looked like pretty decent-sized engines. And unlike the yacht, it looked like its pilot had beached the boat on Loggerhead Key on purpose.

But who was firing? And why weren't these people getting along?

I moved quickly in the darkness and heavy, tropical rain, running on a nondescript sandy pathway that led me in the direction of the lighthouse. I kept a good pace but didn't want my heart rate to skyrocket, which was the only thing keeping me from sprinting towards my destination. If someone was in trouble, every second I spent in pursuit could mean someone's life. But I knew, from years of hunting down enemies, that there was a lot to be said for keeping calm and keeping your wits about you.

As I rounded a patch of prickly pear cacti, I saw the dark outline of five figures moving my direction. They were about three hundred feet away from me as I strayed from the path and took cover behind a large cocoplum plant. As they walked closer, the morning light revealed that it was two guys and three women. The women appeared to be blindfolded, and the two guys were leading them towards the beach, one guy in the front and the other in the back. As they moved closer, I started to see them in more detail. The first guy wore a cutoff black shirt and a pair of soaked jeans and had what appeared to be a revolver in his left hand. The guy in the back wore a dark hoodie and cargo pants and had a stockless AK-47 strapped over his shoulder. They forced the three women to move at a fast pace, cussing at them and pushing them forward. Two of the women looked especially young, with one looking like she was barely in her teens. The ferocious winds violently flapped any articles of loose clothing, and the two guys had their hands raised to cover their faces from sprays of white sand.

I'd heard stories of sex slavery in the Caribbean before. Women on vacation being taken by thugs while out on the water, then transported to Jamaica, Cuba or South America to be eventually sold on the slave market. Most of those women were never seen or heard from again. Still gripping my Sig in my right hand, I slid it into my leg holster.

The group walked right past my position, unable to see me under the cover of the shrubs and darkness. When a loud rumble of thunder echoed across the morning air, I pounced from my hiding place in the shrubs and targeted the trailing guy. Wrapping my arm forcefully around his chest from behind, I pulled him back while stomping my heel into his left calf. His body collapsed and he yelled out in pain and confusion. As he reached for his AK-47, I wrapped my hands around his neck and quickly snapped it sideways. His loud, struggling body went limp in an instant and flattened against the wet sand.

As I reached for my Sig, the other guy turned on his heel. Taking one glace at me, he yelled, "Who the fu—" But his words were cut off by two 9mm rounds lodging in his chest, spitting out splashes of blood through his black shirt into the rain. His body twisted wildly, then crashed into the sand. Both men were dead, and the incident had lasted less than a few seconds.

The three women screamed, and their bodies started to shake after hearing the two gunshots. After taking a quick look around to make sure there weren't any others, I moved towards them slowly, not wanting to scare them any more than they already were.

"It's okay," I said as calmly as I could. "My name is Logan Dodge. I was trying to escape the storm when I heard gunfire and came to investigate." I removed their blindfolds and saw the intense fear in their eyes. One of the women appeared to be in her forties, and I realized she was their mom by the way she held the other two in her arms.

Scared as hell, they stepped away from me when their blindfolds were removed. The mom glanced at the two dead guys on the sand, then turned to me and said, "They were trying to take us away."

"I know," I said, remaining calm but wanting her to hear the seriousness in my voice. Realizing that their hands were zip-tied behind their backs, I slid my dive knife from its sheath and made quick work of the plastic, freeing their hands. "I need you to tell me if there are any more of them. Was it just these two on the island?"

They were all shaking, both from the storm and from the terror of the situation. Though they each had rain slickers on, their clothes were completely soaked.

The mom's eyes suddenly went wide and she stared at me. "My husband." Her voice was shaky and she gasped for breath. "He's in the house. They said they were going to kill him."

Blood surged through my veins. As she spoke, I grabbed the AK-47 from the ground, slung it over my shoulder, then grabbed the other guy's Magnum revolver and stuck it into the back of my belt. Turning around, I looked at the whitewashed house she was referring to and saw that it was just a short distance from the base of the lighthouse.

I moved closer to the mom. "How many are there?"

She shook her head. "I don't know. They blindfolded us."

"Okay," I said. Then, leading them over to a

patch of thick cocoplum shrubs beneath a palm tree, I added, “I need you to stay here. Stay hidden and take care of them, okay?” I nodded to the young girls. After she nodded back, I told her, “I’ll be right back.”

Without another word, I jumped into action, moving swiftly towards the house. It was a small old-style two-story house, surrounded by tall coconut trees that were swaying chaotically in the wind. As I moved towards the back window, I saw a faint glow of light radiating from within. Crouching under the windowsill beside a large propane tank, I peeked over and saw two guys in the living room. One guy was wearing a black leather jacket that was dripping water onto the hardwood floor below. He held a video camera in one hand, and in the other he held what looked like a Magnum revolver, which he kept aimed at the second guy, who was gagged and tied to a chair in the middle of the room.

The guy tied up looked like a professional heavyweight boxer had used him as a punching bag for a few hours. His face was swollen and covered in blood, and he looked so disoriented that I expected he would pass out at any moment. His right leg appeared to be broken, since it was bent sideways at a ninety-degree angle halfway between his foot and his knee. He was wearing a blue polo shirt, brown pants and a pair of boat shoes. Though the sun had risen over the horizon, the thick black clouds blotted out everything but a faint glow, and the only light in the house came from a candle in the kitchen and another on a small table beside the couch in the living room.

The bad guy, after yelling and spitting at the tied-up guy, set his camera on a nearby table and cocked his revolver. The woman had said that they’d planned to kill him, but this looked more like an execution.

Before the guy could level his pistol on his target, I rose from my crouched position, took aim with my Sig and fired off a round. Shattering the glass, it hit the guy right in the side of his head, exploding in a mess of blood and bone. Before his corpse had collapsed onto the hardwood floor, I was throwing my body through the window. Landing on my feet inside what looked like a sorry excuse for a kitchen, I did a quick scan of the house. After I'd checked both floors, making sure there was no one else inside, I turned off the video camera resting on the table, then ran over to the beat-up guy and removed the gag from his mouth.

Grabbing my dive knife, I cut the ropes, which had been tied so tightly that his wrists had turned bright red. I tried to talk to him, tried to get him to stay awake, but I could tell that he was fading in and out of consciousness. Walking over to a small sink, I opened the faucet and was slightly surprised to see water pouring out. Grabbing a nearby bowl, I filled it with water and splashed it over the guy's bloodied face.

His body thrashed, and I had to catch him to keep him from falling out of the chair. Strands of his black hair dripped down, covering the top of his beaten face as he looked around the room, trying to figure out what had happened. He had a decent build, though it was easy to tell from his slightly protruding belly that he spent quite a bit more time on a couch than a treadmill.

"Who are you?" he said, staring at me with intensity in his eyes. Then, looking at the floor, he saw the dead guy lying in a big pool of his own blood with a partially disfigured head. He opened his mouth to continue, but before he could, he was cut off by the slamming of the front door.

In the blink of an eye, my Sig was aimed at the door, ready to pull the trigger at a moment's notice.

"Christian!" a woman's voice cried. The woman, along with her two daughters, ran through the door. She cried frantically as she wrapped her arms around her husband. Part of me wanted to remind her that I'd instructed her to wait in the bushes, but I didn't see what good it would have done.

While embracing his wife and daughters, the guy turned to me and said, "Thank you." His voice was raspy, and I could tell that every breath was a struggle given the pain he was in.

"They were trying to take us away, and this man saved us," one of his daughters said, tears streaking down her face.

"You killed them?" the man asked, his eyes wide and filled with worry. I nodded, and he gave a big sigh of relief. "I was unable to hold them off on my own." He coughed up some blood, cleared his throat and continued, "The four of them surrounded us and caught us by surprise."

My heart sank and my eyes narrowed. Placing my hand on his shoulder, I stared into his dark brown eyes and said, "Did you say four?"

# NINE

His mouth fell open and his eyes grew wide. "Yeah. That's how many there were."

I grabbed my Sig from my leg holster, and as if the fourth guy had read my mind, I heard the sound of gunshots coming from outside the old house. There was a lot of thunder and lightning, but I knew the difference between the sounds they made and the sound of a gunshot. I listened while moving towards the door, but the gunshots were coming from a good distance away, from down by where I'd left my Zodiac.

*Shit*, I thought as I gripped my Sig and sprinted as quickly as I could down the sandy pathway towards my boat. It was about five hundred feet through the bushes and palm trees, and by the time I reached it, I was too late.

The fourth guy had already shoved off on his patrol boat, had the engines running and was gunning it away from the island, his boat crashing over the massive rolling waves. I raised my Sig and took aim. He was far away and moving sideways parallel to the beach, making the shot difficult. When I had him lined up behind the middle white dot of my leveled sight, I fired off two quick shots. The first shattered the port-side windscreen, rocketing inches from his face, and the second hit him square in the chest, causing him to fall sideways. In an instant, his body vanished from view as he fell onto the deck.

While he fell, the guy must have hit the throttles, because the boat was motoring through the waves much slower than before. I kept my Sig aimed at the boat, making sure the guy wasn't going to get back up anytime soon. When I was convinced he was down for the count, I ran over to my Zodiac, which was still tied off along the shrub line. But as I reached it, I realized that it was riddled with bullet holes all across the hull and in both of the pontoons, which had already deflated enough to make the boat unusable. Cursing my unknown assailant, I leaned over and searched what remained of my boat. Not only had the asshole ruined it, but he'd also taken my bags, along with my sniper rifle.

A loud strike of lightning flashed across the morning sky as I looked out over the intense whitecapped ocean. I estimated that the patrol boat was about a half a mile from the beach, and it was being propelled farther and farther away with each passing second. The massive waves and the torrential rainfall, which had only worsened since I'd arrived on Loggerhead, made going after the boat impossible. As much as I hated it, I could only watch as it drifted into the heart of Fay, taking my supplies along with it.

I did a thorough search of my Zodiac, lifting up the deflated pontoons and looking along the edges of the rigid hull. To my surprise, I realized that the guy hadn't taken everything. He'd left my Camelbak, which had my rain slicker, three MREs and my night vision monocular still inside. He'd also left my new spear gun, which I grabbed along with the three spears. Unfortunately, he'd taken all of my extra ammunition, so all I had was the two mags I'd grabbed earlier for my Sig.

After searching every inch of my boat, I put on my rain slicker, strapped on my backpack and headed quickly back towards the house. Though he'd said there were only four, I kept my guard up anyway, with my Sig in my right hand and my spear gun in my left, ready to fire my Sig at a moment's notice while keeping my head on a swivel.

When I opened the front door to the house and entered, the guy, his wife, and their two daughters stared at me as they stood huddled beside an old fireplace with a few dying embers in it. The guy's face was so messed up that I couldn't tell what his expression was, but I assumed he was relieved to see that it was me and not one of the other guys.

Forcing the door shut behind me, I walked over to them as the house creaked and groaned from the powerful winds. The light from the candles illuminated the room, flickering around us.

"Were there any other boats?" I asked, my voice stern and resolute.

The four of them stared at me for a moment, then the guy answered, "Not that we saw. It was just the one." His wife had grabbed a damp towel and was patting her husband's face with it, cleaning off the drying blood. She lifted a glass of water to his lips, and he took one sip before coughing out the attempted second. After clearing his throat, he added,

"Who are you?"

"His name is Logan," his wife said. In the light of the room, I could see that she was pretty, even given the fact that she was worried as hell and soaking wet from head to toe. She had medium-length brunette hair, light hazel eyes and freckles surrounding her nose. She looked about five feet eight inches tall with a lean, athletic build beneath her wet skinny jeans.

"My name is Chris Hale," the guy said. "This is my wife, Cynthia, and my daughters, Jordan and Alex."

I estimated that Jordan was probably fifteen. She had her mother's brown hair, though her eyes were slightly darker. Alex was the youngest daughter, though she looked tall for her age, and she also had brunette hair and hazel eyes. Both girls looked scared out of their minds, and understandably so. They'd been seconds away from being taken away and forced into a life of violence, drugs, and prostitution.

I nodded to each of them, then said, "Well, Chris, it's a little rough out there for a pleasure cruise. What were you doing out on the water in the middle of a tropical storm?"

The old house shook as a violent gust of wind batted against it. Tropical Storm Fay was getting closer, its winds growing more and more powerful with each passing second.

Chris sat in thought for a moment, then, after glancing at his wife, he looked at me and said, "I was running." A loud roar of thunder filled the air. Chris continued, "I'm an attorney, and I represented the state in the case against Benito Salazar, the notorious gang leader who fled Cuba and had been wreaking havoc around the world for over a decade. Before he was taken away to serve his double life sentence, he told me that he would break free and that he would track me down and kill me and my family." He paused for a moment to clear his throat, then continued, "He proclaimed it as he was being taken away from the courtroom. Cursing my name as he stared me down with his evil eyes." He looked away from me, down at his feet. Then, regaining his strength, he said, "Salazar escaped from his Cuban prison two days ago. We were in Cancún and left for the States as quickly as we could."

"You were the prosecutor? And he's sworn revenge against you?" I shook my head. "I'm willing to wager that asshole would've been put away for life no matter what you said."

"Perceptions can be shifted; evidence can be overlooked. If he'd been able to buy off both me and the judge, it's very likely he'd have gotten off pretty easy, or at least much easier than he did. But regardless of that, you must also understand that Salazar is a maniac who tends to disregard logical thinking."

I thought it over for a moment, then said, "So you and the judge were the only ones who didn't budge?"

Chris nodded. "And Salazar had him and his whole family murdered the same day that he escaped from prison."

*Holy shit*, I thought as I looked up at the ceiling, shaking my head. Here I thought this was just another case of piracy in the Caribbean. A rich guy and his beautiful family taken hostage by sex slavers looking to make a quick buck by ruining people's lives. The truth, it seemed, was much worse.

"All flights were grounded, and we thought we

could beat Fay and make it to the States, where a few detectives from Miami were going to meet us," Cynthia said, wiping tears from her face and holding their daughters close to them as she continued to clean off blood. "But we were very, very wrong."

Shifting his beat-up body, Chris said, "They tracked us down and caught up to us about ten miles southwest of here. They yelled at us to stop, and when we didn't, they tore our boat to shreds with automatic gunfire. I had her cruising as fast as she could at forty knots, but they still stayed with us. It wasn't long before I lost control, slammed into a reef and then crashed onto this island."

"How did they find you?" I asked.

Chris sighed. "They had a tracker hidden on the boat. By the time I found it and destroyed it, it was already too late."

"When did you destroy it?"

"Just before crashing," he said as Cynthia continued to wipe the blood from his face and arms, tending to his wounds as best as she could.

*Of course*, I thought.

That meant that Salazar and his gang knew where they were, and he also knew that they were stuck there, at least until the storm passed. And I was stuck with them, I thought, recalling the image of my Zodiac riddled with bullets and resting deflated in the sand. Reaching into my pocket, I pulled out my high-powered Subgear Prolight flashlight and turned it on, shining it around the room. I wanted to see what we had in the house that we could use, and since my satellite phone had been taken, I kept a watchful eye out for anything resembling a radio.

I searched an adjoining room and found nothing but old boxes filled with papers and memorabilia of the island. Upstairs, the house had a small bedroom, which had an old bed, a large chest of drawers and a closet full of park ranger uniforms. Unfortunately, there wasn't anything that would help our situation. I went back downstairs and headed for the front door.

"What are you doing?" Chris asked before I grabbed the doorknob.

Turning to him, I said, "If everything you say is true, then we need to find a way off this island. The Coast Guard will be on alert for stranded vessels and might be able to reach us, even in this storm."

Before he could reply, I opened the door and a powerful gust of wind slammed into me as I quickly stepped through and shut it sternly behind me. Sheets of tropical rain flew sideways across my body as I stepped down onto the beach, heading for the lighthouse. The wooden door at its base was locked, so, rearing back, I slammed my right heel into its center, causing the door to crash open. The first level of the lighthouse appeared to be a small museum with pictures all over the walls of the island, showing how it had looked during its various stages over the years.

I headed up a spiral staircase that seemed to go on forever until I finally reached the top. The blinding lamp rotated in circles, casting a powerful beam of light through the windows around me. It was a great view from up there, and even though the sky was filled with black clouds and thick rain, I was still able to see a good distance out over the horizon in all directions. On the other side of the light, I saw a small metal box, and moving over to it, I pulled open the door, causing its hinges to squeak. Inside, I found a black portable radio and looked it over, but it appeared to be broken as none of the lights came on when I flipped the On switch.

Feeling somewhat defeated and wondering how I could find a way to get in contact with anyone near Key West, I set the broken radio back inside the box and headed back around the light to the top of the staircase. Just as I was about to take the first step, something caught my eye out over the water. Leaning closer to the glass, I let my eyes focus for a moment. Out on the water to the west, on the same line as the wrecked yacht but about a half a mile from the shoreline, there was a boat heading straight for the island. Looking closer, I realized that it was a large boat, probably at least forty feet, and that it was well equipped to take on the massive rolling waves of Tropical Storm Fay. One thing was certain, it sure as hell wasn't the Coast Guard.

# TEN

I flew down the spiral staircase as fast as I could, my heart racing as I tried to think about what to do next. As I reached the door, one certainty dominated my mind: we were outnumbered and outgunned. A shitty situation to be in. Back in the storm, I ran over to the house and barged in through the front door. Cynthia was in the kitchen, running water from the sink into a metal pitcher, and Chris had moved to the nearby couch, where his two daughters sat on either side of him, still overtaken with fear and shock.

Shutting the door behind me, I stormed over to the couch and said, "Chris, I need you to take your wife and daughters upstairs and into the bedroom. Now!"

He looked up at me, his eyes wide and his swollen mouth open. "Why? What is—"

"I need you to do it now!" I said sternly.

Cynthia dropped the pitcher into the sink and ran over to the couch.

"What's going on?" she asked.

Chris looked into my eyes and saw how serious I was. After a moment, he nodded and looked at his wife. "Cynthia, please take the girls upstairs. I'll be up in a moment."

She wrapped her arms around her daughters, and they headed for the staircase. I turned back to Chris when the three of them were out of earshot.

"We're in deep shit," I said. "There's another boat coming this way. A big one. One that probably carries more than four lousy goons."

He gasped as I walked to the other side of the room, crouched down and grabbed the revolver resting on the wooden floor beside the dead guy, whose body they'd moved behind a chair.

Moving back over to Chris, I clicked it open, verifying all six rounds were still loaded, then handed it to him.

"How are you with a gun?"

He reached his bloody hand towards me and grabbed hold of it. "I've been to the range a few times."

I nodded, then glanced at the front door. "If anyone comes through that door that isn't me, you kill them, you hear me?" I could tell that as bad as these guys were, he wasn't as used to the idea of killing someone as I was, so I tried to give him some perspective. "Remember, these guys will kill you and do far worse things to your wife and daughters if given the chance. Do not give them that chance. Do not show them mercy. Understand?"

He nodded, then grunted. "Those assholes beat the shit out of me. I can barely stand. How am I supposed to help you fight them off?"

"Just aim at the door, alright?" I said, then

grabbed the AK-47, which was still slung over my shoulder, and checked the magazine. Seeing that it had a full thirty rounds ready to go, I jammed the mag back into the rifle and added, "I'll try to keep them from reaching the house. But just in case."

I slid my Sig from my leg holster and exchanged magazines, loading in the fifteen-round mag and placing the one with ten shots left in the holster strap. Moving into the kitchen, I licked my fingers and put out the candle. Then I moved the other candle onto the coffee table beside the front door. This made it so Chris could easily see who was coming in through the door, but they would have a hard time seeing him.

I turned back to Chris and said, "Don't hesitate," then grabbed the doorknob, twisted it and pulled open the front door. The strong winds whistled into the room, causing the door to slam shut behind me. The rain beat down against my body as I sprinted off the front porch, then headed onto the sandy pathway that led to the western beach. When I was just a few hundred feet away from the massive crashing waves, I took cover behind a thick patch of railroad vines, interwoven around various green shrubs, and watched as the boat cruised full throttle over roaring whitecaps towards the beach.

I took a quick look around, knowing I had less than thirty seconds before they'd reach the shoreline. I crawled along the thick vines and hid alongside a small sandbank, behind a cluster of majesty palms that were about twenty feet away from the path. Close enough for me to pounce on them but far away enough for them not to see me. I watched as the boat rose up and down over the waves, listening as the sounds of the engine roared, propelling it forward. It was a rugged storm chaser just like the other one had been, though much larger.

I glanced at my dive watch and was surprised to see that it was just past 0700 as the sky was still dark, the black clouds of Tropical Storm Fay blocking out the sun. A moment later, the boat sped up and then slammed its hull into the beach, its momentum forcing it forward. When it stopped, I watched six guys jump out and counted at least two more still on the boat, their heads peeking over the windscreen.

They did a quick search of the yacht and what remained of my sorry excuse for a Zodiac, then headed over to the path leading towards the house. They looked a lot like the other guys, typical thugs armed with Uzis and AK-47s. The six of them stuck together and moved quickly up the path. When they were about a hundred feet away from me, a loud crack of thunder rattled my eardrums and shook the ground. The six guys slowed and raised their hands to prevent a strong gust of wind from slamming sheets of rain and fine sand into their faces. That was my window.

I holstered my Sig and grabbed my AK. Rising up from my crouching position, I took aim at the group, then held down the trigger. The rounds exploded out the end of the barrel, rattling the stock, which was pressed hard against my right shoulder. The stream of bullets pierced the bodies of the unsuspecting thugs as I shifted my aim from one guy to the next. One by one they flew backward, arms flailing and blood splattering in all directions.

In less than a second, I had four of them on the ground, their bodies riddled with bullets. The two guys farthest from me, however, had dropped to the beach and rolled for cover on the other side of the pathway. Before I could take them out, they'd grabbed their weapons and fired off a few shots in my general direction, forcing me to drop back onto my chest as bullets whizzed around me, the occasional round soaring just a few feet over the top of my head. They stopped firing for a moment and yelled out to their buddies back on the boat.

Sliding the shoulder strap off my body and dropping the AK to the ground, I crawled as fast as I could along the pathway towards the house, putting as much distance between myself and where the two guys had last spotted me as I could. I found a good spot behind a thick patch of various shrubs and waited, watching closely as the two guys rose and walked slowly towards the place where I'd left my AK. Another guy suddenly appeared from the beach. He looked a lot bigger than the other guys and had two Uzis, one in each hand.

After searching the area and finding my AK on the ground, the three guys split up to look for me. Keeping their distance, they moved slowly through the thick underbrush, making their way towards the house. One of them, a tall skinny guy with a faded ballcap over his head and a drenched windbreaker, shuffled his way in my direction. He had a twelve-gauge in his hands and what looked like a grenade clipped to his belt. Keeping a watchful eye, he crept right beside me. I knew that, given my position under the thick shrubs, along with the dark gray skies and the heavy rains and strong winds, it would be almost impossible for him to see me. I trusted my camouflage, keeping my body perfectly still and allowing the guy to move within five feet of my position.

Suddenly, a powerful gust of wind kicked up a layer of fine sand right into his body. He raised an arm to shield his face, and as he did so, I made my move. With my Sig still strapped securely to my holster, I reached for my dive knife instead. Gripping it with my cold wet hands, I slid it from my leg sheath and sprang to my feet. Before the guy could see me, I had my left arm wrapped around his face and, jerking his body back, I stabbed the sharp stainless-steel blade of my knife right through his neck. Blood flowed out as I pulled it free, then forced his shaking body to the ground. He didn't make a sound, and within seconds, his body became motionless in the shrubs.

Wiping my blade against his drenched cargo pants, I cleaned off the blood, then slid it back into its sheath and took a quick look around, making sure that no one had seen me. The two other guys had yet to realize that their buddy was missing and continued through the storm towards the house. Grabbing the dead guy's shotgun, I made sure it was locked and loaded, then took aim at the nearest guy. He spotted me just as I pulled the trigger, sending a swarm of lead pellets into his chest. His body launched backward, blood spraying into the rain, then slammed onto the beach.

The big guy with the two Uzis in his hands saw what had happened and yelled out as he took aim at me. But before he could, I already had him in my sights, shifting over with my twelve-gauge in the blink of an eye. A few shots from his Uzis rattled off in my general direction as I pumped the shotgun, ejecting the spent shell and chambering a fresh one, then fired the barrage of pellets straight towards his head.

Blood and bone exploded out as the big guy fell to the ground, his Uzis firing a few rounds straight into the air before dropping from his hands onto the sand. I ran over to the dead thugs and saw that both of their corpses were sprawled out, covered in blood, and their limbs were positioned unnaturally around them. When it was clear that neither of them would ever be getting up again, I turned my sights to the boat.

Reaching down, I grabbed my AK-47, switching it with the twelve-gauge, and ran towards the beach. I kept the rifle aimed forward just in case another guy had decided to come and join in the fight. When I reached the area where the thick shrubbery transitioned into sandy beach, I looked towards the loud crashing waves and saw the large storm chaser. It was back in the water, its engines roaring wildly as it struggled to propel itself backwards into the powerful swells. The guy left on the boat must have heard all the commotion, gotten spooked and decided to get the hell out of there as fast as he could.

Throwing the AK on the ground, I sprinted for the boat, my feet sinking into the wet sand, then splashing through the shallow foamy water. I timed my strides as best as I could as the bow of the boat rocked wildly up and down, giving myself the best chance to make a move. Just before I'd reached the boat, the pilot spotted me through the drenched windscreen. He tried to force the boat back, giving it even more gas to try and get away from me. I was waist-deep when I saw a massive wave barreling towards the stern of the boat. With the bow in a dip, I took one more step, then forced my body up out of the water, extending my arms and wrapping my hands around the metal railing.

My hands became vise grips as the massive wave forced the stern to rocket upwards, followed swiftly after by the bow. My body jerked skyward as the salty water crashed over me, covering my body along with the entire bow. As the wave passed, the pilot forced the throttles back even more, seeing that I was still holding on. The boat picked up speed, bouncing over wave after wave, and when we were about five hundred feet from shore, he eased the reverse throttles and turned her around. Holding on tight, I used the momentum of the turn to swing my body up over the railing and landed on the metal bow. Glancing at the pilothouse, I saw that the guy inside had picked up his gun and had it leveled in my direction. I dove out of sight, barely avoiding the bullets that shattered the windscreen and sparked off the deck beside me.

Once the boat was turned around, with its bow facing the open ocean, the pilot forced the throttles forward. The sudden change in speed and direction whiplashed my body against the starboard railing, almost knocking me off the boat completely. Regaining my balance, I pulled my Sig from its holster and crouched down beside the pilothouse. As the boat started to pick up speed, I rose from my position, took aim, and fired a shot, the bullet shattering the side window and lodging in the guy's chest. He yelled out in pain as his body fell sideways, then collapsed to the deck.

I slammed open the solid metal door and leveled my Sig at his head, ready to blow his brains out at a moment's notice. With my right hand gripping my Sig, I reached over to the throttles with my left and eased them back, slowing the boat to about fifteen knots.

"Start talking, asshole!" I said, pressing the barrel of my Sig into his forehead. "How many more of you are out here?"

The guy looked slightly older than the other guys that were on the island, maybe in his early forties judging by his balding head. He had dark tanned skin and deep brown eyes that were shooting daggers at me as he struggled to catch his breath.

"You dumbass," he said, keeping his hands pressed against his bleeding chest. "You think you can protect them?" He shook his head, and his lips contorted to form an evil smile. "We're just the tip of the damn spear. Salazar will get his way. If he has to blow up that entire island, he will kill that family."

"Not while I'm still breathing, he won't," I fired back. The boat continued to jerk up and down as we cruised into the storm.

The guy sighed deeply and looked up at me with his dark eyes. "Then I'll see you in hell." He shot me another evil smile that I couldn't stand to look at.

With my Sig still pressed against his skull, I pulled the trigger, splattering his blood against the windscreen. As his body went limp, his left hand, which I realized had been making a fist, opened up and I watched as a plastic switch with a red flickering light fell to the deck.

*Shit*, I thought as I turned around and took a few quick strides through the door towards the aft end of the boat. Digging my right heel into the transom, I launched my body overboard, and as I flew through the air, a loud explosion rattled behind me, propelling me forward with a powerful shockwave. My eardrums screamed and pieces of plastic and metal slammed into me as I crashed through the surface of the whitecapped water.

# ELEVEN

The warm tropical water engulfed me, and for a moment the world turned quiet as a surge of pain radiated through my body. The force of the explosion had almost knocked me unconscious, and the heat from the bursting flames singed a few hairs on my head. My ears rang loudly as if I'd just been in a room after a concussion grenade had gone off, and for a moment, I almost forgot where I was as I swirled underwater. Shaking it off and getting my bearings, I kicked for the surface, breaking through and returning to a violent world of heavy rains, massive waves, cracks of lightning and roaring thunder in an instant.

My head still delirious from the impact and my ears still ringing, I swam towards the burning rubble that was all that remained of the boat. Most of it was in pieces and either sank to the bottom or floated violently on the whitecapped surface around me. When it was clear that I wasn't gonna be able to salvage anything useful from the wreck, I turned towards the shore, feeling somewhat dejected. That boat had been our only ticket off the island, and since it had been destroyed, we had no choice but to stay.

I utilized the combat side stroke as I kicked and pulled my way through the rough water, diving down every now and then to escape the torrential rain or to avoid a large wave from throwing my body around like a rag doll. After spending a few minutes swimming underwater, I'd rise up on the crest of a wave and look forward, making sure that I was staying on course. It was about half of a mile to the island, and unfortunately, I had to buck a current that was pulling me out to sea. With the current slowing my progress and the strong winds and waves to deal with, it took me over an hour of intense swimming to reach the shore. When my feet struck the sand and I trudged through the crashing waves up to the shrub line, my body was so fatigued that I felt like collapsing onto the beach. But there was no time for that.

Instead, I headed straight for the yacht. Climbing aboard, I entered through the main hatch into the salon. Seawater was pouring in through the sides and up through the cracked hull as I searched the forward cabin. Under a pile of broken paneling, I found a large blue roller bag. I emptied its contents onto the bed and carried it outside. Hauling it over the side of the yacht in one hand, I did a quick scan up and down the beach, then out over the horizon. From my vantage point on the beach, I couldn't see very far. The waves were too choppy and the sky too dark. Gripping the bag tightly, I moved along the path towards the four corpses lying beside each other, searching them one by one for anything and everything useful.

Two of them had Uzis, one had a Beretta M9 and the fourth had a sawed-off shotgun along with an incendiary grenade. Gathering all the weapons, I threw them into the roller bag, then moved on to the bodies near the shrubs. I picked up the shotgun and the AK-47, along with an extra magazine, then searched the big guy whose face I'd splattered into a mushy mess of blood and grated skin. Grabbing both of his Uzis, I flipped over his body and found two M26 frag grenades strapped to the back of his belt. Setting them inside the bag along with the Uzis, I also found a small black radio and stowed it inside with the weapons.

After searching all the bodies, I carried the blue roller bag over my shoulder towards the house. The wind had picked up even more, shoving sheets of fine sand and raindrops against my body. I knew that it had to be at least sixty miles per hour, with gusts in the seventies. I moved to the front of the house and stepped up onto the porch. Knocking on the front door, I cracked open the door a few inches and yelled at Chris, telling him not to shoot me before stepping inside. He was still sprawled out on the couch, the revolver lodged in his right hand, pointed at the floor. He looked relieved to see me as I shut and locked the door behind me, water dripping from my clothes and onto the hardwood floor.

"I heard the gunshots," he said, worry plastered across his beat-up face. "How many were there?"

Walking into the kitchen, I bent down, picked up the roller bag and set it on the kitchen table. "Eight," I said, unzipping the bag and grabbing the radio from inside. Holding it up to my face, I twisted the On switch and watched as a green light lit up. Scanning through the channels, I quickly realized that it was a low-frequency radio, designed for short-range communications. Clearly, the big guy had grabbed it so he could talk to the guy on the boat, not anyone off the island.

"Eight? You killed them all?" When I didn't reply, he continued, "Does it work?"

I turned towards him and saw that his eyes were staring intently at the radio in my hands. "Yeah, but I doubt we'll be able to get ahold of anyone this far away from Key West." Walking over to the couch, I threw the radio into his lap. "Mess around with that for a while. I gotta take care of these weapons and then move all the bodies."

In the basement of the house, I found an old chest filled with various papers and knickknacks. Emptying its contents, I brought it upstairs and filled it with the dead guys' guns. Before heading back outside, I grabbed one of the AK-47s, checked its magazine to make sure it was full, then slung it over my shoulder. Chris was tinkering with the radio as I opened the front door and headed back out into the storm. Palm leaves and bushes tumbled in the wind and loose sand scattered in violent sheets, building up against the southwest side of the house.

Grabbing the corpses by their ankles, I dragged each of them to a spot surrounded by thick cocoplum bushes and palm trees that were all taller than I was. A place where, given the darkness of the sky, it would be almost impossible for anyone to see that they were there. When I finished with the last guy, I grunted, took a long, deep breath and shielded my face from the rain. Back inside the house, I grabbed one of my MREs and cut open the plastic pouch of food using my dive knife. Then, I added water into the pouch, which created a chemical reaction when it interacted with a small pad of magnesium, salt, and iron dust. This reaction was used to create a flameless heater that in turn allowed deployed soldiers to have the comfort of a warm meal in a matter of minutes.

A few moments later, I started to smell the garlic chicken with potato cubes and corn, causing my mouth to water. Glancing at my watch, I saw that it was past ten. I'd spent over an hour moving the corpses and an hour swimming in the raging ocean before that, making my body scream at me to take it easy and chill out for a moment. I filled a plastic gallon jug I'd found in the pantry with water from the faucet.

Gripping my steaming MRE in one hand, I looked over at Chris and said, "You want one?"

Chris shook his head, "I don't have much of an appetite."

Shrugging, I headed towards him. "I saw some canned food in the pantry if you change your mind." Then, casting my gaze up to the ceiling, I added, "It would be good for them to eat something. Might take their minds off things."

When he didn't reply, I set my MRE and my AK-47 on the table, then walked up the creaky old wooden stairs and knocked softly on the bedroom door.

"Who is it?" I heard Cynthia's voice say faintly over the sounds of the storm outside.

"It's Logan," I replied calmly.

A moment later, I heard the sliding of metal as she unlocked and opened the door. Cynthia appeared in the doorway, her clothes and hair still slightly damp. She still had fear in her light hazel eyes as she examined me from head to toe. Her two daughters were on the bed behind her, bundled together under a quilt.

"There's some food downstairs if any of you are hungry," I said.

After a moment's pause, she said, "Are you alright?"

I nodded, then, spotting a pair of binoculars on the windowsill inside the bedroom, I said, "Can I get those?"

Turning around, Cynthia saw what I was referring to, then walked over and grabbed them. Her daughters told her that they were hungry as she carried it back over to the door and handed it to me.

"Thanks," I said before turning around and heading down the stairs.

I grabbed my AK and slung it over my shoulder, then gripped my MRE as I moved over to where Chris was sitting on the couch with his broken right leg propped up on an old cushion.

"Any luck with that thing?" I said, motioning at the radio in his lap.

He shook his head. "There's nothing in range."

I reached out my hand and said, "Here, let me see it."

He handed it to me, and I switched it off and clipped it to my belt, untucking and covering it with the end of my green rain slicker to keep it as dry as I could.

As I moved for the door, Chris said, "Where are you going?"

I pointed through the window at the lighthouse, where every few seconds, a beam of light flickered through the rain-splattered glass. "Up there. It's the best vantage point."

"You really think you can hold these guys off on your own?" he said. "You've obviously got some training, but what happens when Salazar decides to stop messing around and sends a hundred guys here? How could you possibly take on that many by yourself?"

"I'm working on it," I fired back. "Just do your part. You're our last line of defense."

I was out the door and back in the storm before he replied. The last thing I needed was for someone to remind me how high the odds were stacked against us.

# TWELVE

From the top of the lighthouse, I could see for miles in all directions, even with the storm swirling black clouds and thick sheets of rain through the air. I leaned back into a blue folding chair I'd found in a small storage space about halfway up the stairs and opened my MRE, allowing a puff of steam to rise out and dissipate inside the small space. Grabbing an old metal fork, I dug in, cooling off the first few bites before throwing them down the hatch. Unlike most people I'd met in the Navy, I actually enjoyed MREs for the most part. I guess it was because my dad had always brought them along on our camping trips just in case the fishing or hunting didn't pan out.

This one was particularly good, and I ate it in less than two minutes, not realizing just how hungry I was. The protein, carbs and over twelve hundred calories were just what my body needed and quelled my groaning stomach. Grabbing my jug of water, I took a few long swigs to wash it all down before gripping the old binoculars and scanning the horizon. Big raindrops splattered violently against the glass, making the image blurry, but I knew that I'd still be able to spot a boat heading our way. Surprisingly, I could see pretty clearly the red brick walls of Fort Jefferson three miles to the East. Just northwest of Fort Jefferson, both Hospital Key and Middle Key were completely covered with water, swallowed by massive whitecapped swells.

Even with the ferocious winds beating against the side of the lighthouse, the old structure didn't make the slightest sound. I didn't know a lot about the history of Loggerhead Key, but I did know that the lighthouse had been constructed in 1858, which meant that it had been standing for exactly one hundred and fifty years. In all those years, I'm sure it had seen hundreds of hurricanes and tropical storms, many of which I was sure were much worse than Fay. The truth was, if I was going to be stranded on an island in the middle of a tropical storm, a lighthouse was probably the best place to be.

I leaned back in my chair, my head just a few feet below the spinning light. Since I could only see half of the horizon at a time, I shifted my chair to face west. That way I could see the yacht and any boats coming near that side of the island. I'd twist my body every few minutes and stretch my neck behind me, making sure there was no activity on the other side that I was missing.

By the time noon came around, Fay appeared to be dying off a little, swirling northeast towards the Panhandle. At the rate it was going, I estimated that she'd be clear of Loggerhead later in the evening. Reaching for the radio that sat idly on the ground beside my feet, I switched it on and did a quick scan of the frequencies, listening for any sign of a good signal. When I didn't hear anything, I turned it off and set it back where it was, trying to minimize the drain of the battery as much as I could. In a normal distress situation, I would have set the radio to channel sixteen, the channel designated by the International Telecommunications Union for distress and safety, and made a full report of our situation. But it wasn't a normal distress situation, and I didn't know who else might have been listening in.

At a few minutes past 1300, I was leaning against the glass, just stretching my legs, when I heard footsteps coming from the spiral stairway. Instinctively, my right hand wrapped around my Sig and slid it free of its holster. But as the footsteps moved closer, I realized that they were far too light for it to be a grown man coming up the stairs. I returned my Sig to the holster strapped to my leg just as Cynthia's head poked up into the small space. She looked better and slightly more relaxed than before.

Her light brown hair was dry, having been shielded from the rain by the hood of a parka she must have found somewhere inside the old house. In one hand, she held a plastic container of steaming food, and in the other a stainless-steel mug, its contents hidden by a small lid.

Glancing at me with her light hazel eyes, she said, "I thought you might be getting hungry again." I smiled at her as she took a step closer, set the mug on the ground and pried open the container. I was surprised at how good the smell was as she stirred the food around with a fork and then handed it to me. "There's only canned foods in the house. But they did have a pretty good selection of seasonings, so I made do."

"Thank you," I said as I looked down at what appeared to be a mixture of rice, black beans and some sort of meat. Taking a bite, I was taken aback by the flavor and couldn't help but dive right back in for another forkful.

"Not bad?" she said, eyeing me with her eyebrows raised.

I smiled. "It's delicious. You should open a restaurant. If you can cook this with just canned food, I'd be curious what you could do when the ingredients are fresh."

"Funny you should say that," she said, grinning and handing me the mug.

I wrapped my hand around it, feeling the warm liquid inside. "What, you already do?"

She nodded. "Just opened my second restaurant in Miami a few months ago. It's the reason we're down here in the first place. Chris wanted to celebrate by taking us to one of our favorite resorts in Cancún. We'd been enjoying our time for a few days when Tropical Storm Fay changed course. We tried to switch to an earlier flight, but all flights had been grounded. It was just a few hours after we'd decided to get a hotel inland and outlast the storm that Chris got a phone call from a detective he'd worked with in Havana. He'd told Chris that Salazar had escaped. It was just a few hours after that phone call that we found out that Judge Wallace and his family had been murdered in their home in the Venetian Islands in Miami."

While listening to her, I took a few more bites and washed them down with sips of the hot coffee from the mug. The steaming liquid felt good as it flowed down into my body, and I felt like I could already notice the effects of the caffeine.

"Then that's when they came after you?"

"Yes," she said. "At the hotel. We barely managed to escape on that beautiful Regal yacht from Marina Hacienda del Mar, which was just down the beach from our resort. It belongs to Chris's uncle, and he'd always let us use it whenever we visited. Chris and I had always been avid boaters. We would have reached the Lower Keys in less than twelve hours if it hadn't been for those gang members."

I took a few more bites and another sip of coffee while mulling over her words. After a few minutes, I finished the food and she reached for the container. "Thanks again," I said. "And for the coffee too. You're a lifesaver."

She smiled as she grabbed the empty container from my hands. "No, you are." She paused a moment as she stared out over the horizon. Taking in a deep breath, she let it all out, then said, "Look, since Chris's stubborn hypermasculine ass probably won't ever say it—thank you for everything you've done. We'd all be dead or worse if you hadn't shown up."

I looked into her light hazel eyes as she spoke. I liked her. She was strong and stern but also had a charming Southern flair in the way that she spoke and in her mannerisms.

"I'm just doing what any honorable man would do," I said.

She shook her head. "You're doing what almost no man would do."

I looked away from her momentarily to scan the horizon and make sure there weren't any more boats approaching. When I looked back at her, she'd turned around and was heading back down the stairs.

A few more uneventful hours passed, and I used the time to clean the sand from my Sig and the AK-

47, letting my mind wander to everything from my time as a kid to the last few months I'd spent with Sam. Despite how hard I'd tried, I couldn't get her out of my mind. I guess it would just take time, but deep down, I knew that I'd never fully get over her. That I'd felt things for her that I'd never felt for anyone else before. I also thought about Angelina, the fiery blonde badass who I'd worked alongside many times over the years during various jobs around the world. I thought about how she'd saved my ass while I was fighting Black Venom, taking down Marco with a seemingly impossible shot from her sniper rifle. I hadn't heard anything from her since she'd taken a job in Africa, and I hadn't seen her since the evening we'd celebrated finding the Aztec treasure with Nazari at Pete's restaurant. I found myself worrying about her, even though she was arguably the most lethal woman on the planet.

By 1800, as the sun started to drop down into the ocean, Tropical Storm Fay had almost completely abated. The rains had dissipated, and the majority of the black clouds had blown northeast towards the mainland of Florida. Though the winds had died down, which was clear from observing the shaking coconut trees below and the whitecaps over the ocean, I estimated that they were still blowing at over thirty miles per hour. Regardless, we'd made it through the storm and had to either find a way to get rescued or somehow find a way off Loggerhead. The problem was that there was only one group of people who knew that we were stranded on that island, and let's just say that they weren't the type of guys you wanted to encounter in a dark alley. They were the breed of evil men who would spill innocent blood without hesitation. The kind who would torture and kill all five of us if given the chance—and they'd do it with smiles on their faces.

Half an hour later, as the western sky was lit up in various shades of reds, yellows, and pinks, Cynthia returned with another container of food. She smiled as she handed it to me, and I thanked her again, though she just waved me off, telling me it was the least that she could do. We sat in silence for a few minutes as I enjoyed her food. It was similar to what she'd brought me before, but I could tell that she'd added some additional spices to the mix. Like earlier, I downed the food quickly and watched as the sun disappeared out over the horizon.

When I finished eating, I asked her how her husband and daughters were doing, and she told me that they were doing as good as could be expected. We talked for a while and I was surprised to learn that she had once wanted to be a doctor. She had spent one year at medical school before dropping out after getting pregnant with Jordan. She'd learned enough in that year to take care of Chris's wounds, bandaging him up and making sure he didn't get an infection.

"He'll be fine," she said. "But he won't be moving under his own strength anytime soon."

Looking at my watch, I saw that it was almost 2000, meaning we'd been talking for an hour and a half and I'd been keeping watch at the top of the lighthouse for a little over twelve hours. Grabbing the empty container, she thanked me again for everything and headed back down the stairs.

A few hours later, as my eyelids were growing heavier and heavier, she appeared once more, this time with a thin quilt wrapped around her body.

"I'm here to relieve you," she said, sitting on the ground beside my foldout chair. "You need to get some sleep," she added, her worried eyes meeting mine and noticing how fatigued I was from the long day. "You'll be no good if you don't."

I thought it over for only a moment. Though I wanted badly to take her advice and at least get a few hours down, I couldn't bring myself to do it. What if while I was snoozing, she fell asleep as well? Salazar's thugs could sneak up on us, surround us and take us down with little if any retaliation. No, I couldn't take that chance.

Shaking my head, I said, "I'm fine. But could you bring me another cup of coffee?"

She sighed. "You're not fine. How can you be? You spent all day fighting those guys and its after midnight. You need to get some rest. I'll keep a lookout."

Adjusting one of my legs, I glanced up at her and said, "You know, I was once on an extended deployment in the Middle East."

"You were in the Army?"

"No. Navy."

She looked at me, smiled and said, "That's what I thought. You're a SEAL, aren't you?"

I nodded. "Anyway, after six months abroad, while hunting a group of Taliban in the Arma Mountains in southeastern Afghanistan, my entire platoon had gone over seventy-two hours without a night's sleep, spending most of those hours in intense combat and trekking through mountains with eighty pounds of gear on our backs." I paused for a moment, then chugged down the rest of my coffee. "We didn't make excuses and we didn't slip up. If we had, we'd all have been dead." When she didn't say anything, I held out my empty mug to her. "Could you bring me another cup of coffee?"

After a brief moment, she nodded, grabbed my mug and headed back downstairs. Five minutes later, she returned with a large thermos and handed it to me. "That should tide you over."

I thanked her again as she walked down the spiral staircase and eventually back into the house a few hundred feet away. I untwisted the cap and took a few sips before standing up to stretch my legs. Staring out over the western horizon, a few miles out from where the yacht lay wrecked on the beach, I saw something that caught my eye. It was foreign to the surface of the ocean. Grabbing my night vision monocular out of my Camelbak, I took a better look at the dark object and saw that it was a ship. It appeared to be a large salvage vessel, and it was heading straight for the island.

# THIRTEEN

As the salvage ship drew nearer and the sky grew darker, I switched over to my night vision monocular to get a better look at it. It was about two hundred feet long and was equipped with a helipad, a radio tower and a massive crane that branched out at the stern. It looked old, its bulkheads and the visible portions of its hull covered in rust. On its side, the name Estrella Cubana was painted in faded white letters, contrasting against the dark blue hull. Near the crane at the aft end of the ship, I counted three skiffs strapped down in a row, and on the helipad sat what looked like a Bell 206 twin-bladed single-engine transport helicopter.

The ship continued until it was about half a mile from the northern side of the island, then dropped its rusty anchor with a big splash. There were a lot of guys lumbering about on the deck, though from so far away and with the limited magnification of my night vision monocular, I couldn't make out their faces.

One thing was clear, however—they sure as hell weren't a rescue team.

For the next hour, I watched them under the dark, cloudless sky that was full of twinkling stars. I never took my eyes off the ship for more than a second, and at about one thirty in the morning, it looked like they were planning to make a move. There were guys prepping one of the boats, dressed in full body armor and armed with AKs, M-16s, and submachine guns. I watched as they loosened the straps holding it down, then clipped it onto the end of the crane, lifted it up and lowered it over and down onto the water below. *Shit*, I thought as I counted eight guys boarding the boat, which looked like a twenty-foot military-grade black rigid-hull inflatable.

As they fired up the engine, I threw my AK over my shoulder, dropped my monocular into my cargo shorts pocket and ran down the spiral stairs. From half a mile away, it would take them about a minute, maybe two at the most, to reach the beach. Barging through the door of the lighthouse at the base of the stairs, I ran across the sand and entered the house. The living room was still lit by a single dying candle, which rested on the coffee table beside the couch. Chris had moved over to a dusty recliner; Cynthia and the girls were all seated on the couch beside him, huddled beneath a quilt. Chris had gripped his revolver when he saw the door open and was just about to raise it in my direction before he realized that it was me. I was glad to see he was so alert but didn't have time to tell him so.

All four of them woke up and stared at me as I shut the door behind me. "Back upstairs, now," I said, walking towards the kitchen while looking over at Cynthia and motioning towards the old staircase.

Seeing the hard expression on my face, the three of them jumped to their feet and moved towards the stairs.

"What's going on?" Chris asked, trying to sit up in the recliner and wincing in pain. "Are they back?"

I didn't answer. I didn't want to frighten the girls.

Before reaching the bottom step, Cynthia stopped, turned around and stepped towards me in the kitchen. "Logan—"

"Make sure you lock the bedroom door," I said as I grabbed the chest I'd filled with weapons and slammed it onto the kitchen table.

She nodded. "I know how to use a gun." She had short, quick breaths in between her words. "My dad was a hunter."

Opening the chest, I reached inside and pulled out the Beretta I'd found in one of the dead thugs' hands the previous day. Sliding out the mag to give it a quick check, I slid it back in, verified the safety was on and handed it to her.

"Fifteen rounds," I said while grabbing one of the frag grenades from inside the chest and clipping it onto my belt. "Make sure you're both ready. I'll come back inside and call your names when the island's clear."

She nodded and moved swiftly back to the base of the stairs, joining her two daughters as they helped Chris up the old wooden steps.

"I hope to hell you don't have to use it," I said to myself when they were out of earshot.

Digging inside the chest a few seconds more, I grabbed the extra magazine for my Sig, which I'd filled with 9mm rounds from one of the MAC-10 Uzis. Then, knowing that I'd have to take out at least a few of them quietly, I grabbed my new spear gun, along with the leather sleeve storing two sharpened steel spears.

When I was satisfied, I closed the chest, set it back inside the pantry and shut the two folding doors. Moving for the front door, I knew that I didn't have much time before they'd make it to the beach. I licked my thumb and index finger, then pressed them together, extinguishing the candle before grabbing the doorknob. Once outside, I shut the door behind me and ran to the beach, keeping my footsteps light and listening for any sign of the thugs. As I reached the beach, I heard the sound of their outboard and the distant splashing of their wake as they motored closer to the island. Grabbing my monocular, I watched as their fast black rigid-hull inflatable boat cruised right alongside the island, moving northeast, parallel with the shore.

I was amazed at how calm the world around me had become. The sky was so clear I could see countless stars dotting the night sky, including the celestial formations Orion, Crux, and Centaurus. The winds had died down to nothing more than an occasional soft breeze against my face. Out on the water, the roaring whitecapped seas had been replaced with a dead calm, the surface as smooth as ice.

I watched as the boat motored slowly along the island, just a few hundred feet from the beach. The guys on board appeared to be scoping out the place, so I kept low and out of their line of sight. Clearly, they were more experienced than the guys I'd previously faced off against. They didn't just rush in with their guns blazing and their brains switched off. They were formulating a tactic to take me down, to take all of us down, as effectively as possible.

A few steps from the sandy path, I saw a small pool of muddy water where the bushes met the white sand. Making my way over to it, I dug my hands into the murky mess, cupped scoops of mud and covered my face with it. Then I moved on to my forearms and legs, making sure every inch of my tanned Caucasian skin was covered. I threw a few splashes over my shirt and shorts as well to blend in better, then directed my attention back to the boat. A moment later, as their boat neared the northern tip of the island, they turned on a brilliant spotlight, sending a streak of white light towards the dark island.

Scanning the beam back and forth along the beach, they turned inland and beached their boat in the surf. I watched as four of the guys jumped out, then pushed the boat back into the water. The boat continued down the beach as the four guys moved together up towards the shrub line. After grouping together for a moment, the four guys split up and moved slowly towards the center of the island, switching on their flashlights and scanning the area ahead of them thoroughly before pressing on. It was obvious that these guys were contract killers. Mercenaries like me. Real warriors. I took in a deep breath and crawled a few feet closer to the sandy path, my body camouflaged by the shrubs surrounding me and the mud covering my body.

For a brief moment, I thought about Rainsford from Richard Connell's *The Most Dangerous Game*. How he, too, had the odds stacked against him while being hunted on an island, much like I was. It had always been a favorite story of mine, and at that moment I knew exactly what it felt like.

I watched as the guy closest to me shined his flashlight back and forth with each step. Like the others, he was wearing a full set of body armor, which included a bulletproof vest and helmet. He held an M4A1 assault rifle in his hands, a flashlight mounted to the end of it. Slowly, I reached for one of the spears and quietly loaded it into my spear gun, drawing back the bands, which had a combined draw strength of over eighty pounds. Though it was designed to be shot underwater, I was confident that it would do the trick of taking him out quietly if I got my aim right. When the guy was within fifty feet of my location, he spoke momentarily into the radio built into his helmet, letting the others know that his area was all clear. He still hadn't seen me when I took aim and pulled the trigger, launching the steel spear through the air at over one hundred and fifty feet per second. The sharp tip struck through the guy's neck, right between his helmet and body armor, piercing through to the other side and spraying out blood. He gagged for a second before collapsing to the sand.

I crawled quickly through the thick railroad vines and grass, shuffling past the dead body and towards the second guy. They were spaced out a few hundred feet apart, and it was only a matter of time before they'd notice he was down or tried to radio him, only to hear silence. Hiding on the other side of a small sandbank, I waited for the second guy to trek over it, keeping perfectly still. As he stood over me, he shined his flashlight towards his dead comrade and froze for a moment before reaching for his earpiece. Before he could speak a word, I shifted my body around and snapped my right foot forcefully into his legs, hinging his body and slamming his head into the sand. As he reached for his weapon, I grabbed my dive knife and launched myself on top of him, stabbing the blade through his heart as I kept my hand over his mouth to keep him from making a sound.

Just as his body was going lifeless, a third guy appeared over the sandbank. He shined his flashlight right into my face and fired off a few rounds as I dislodged my bloody dive knife, reared it back and threw it straight at him. His bullets rattled around me, shooting up piles of sand as my knife stabbed into the center of his face. Blood sprayed out as he groaned, his body jerking backward and his M4 exploding rounds straight into the night sky. I sprang to my feet and sprinted towards him as his body collapsed onto the sand.

Using the sandbank as cover, I grabbed my AK and held it tightly pressed against my shoulder. As I looked over the sand, I saw the fourth guy shining his light in my direction. Just as he spotted me, he sent a stream of bullets my way, forcing me to drop down onto my stomach to take cover. As the rounds buzzed just over my head, I rolled to my right, tumbling through the sand as fast as I could. During a brief ceasefire, I popped two, took aim at the guy as he kneeled beside a small majesty palm to reload, and held the AK's trigger. A line of 7.62x32mm bullets tore through the quiet dark sky, making contact first with his lower half, then tearing through his upper body, penetrating his armor and shaking his body violently. Once I'd put about ten rounds into him, I let go of the trigger, and his body fell backward onto a large prickly pear plant.

There was no need to run over and verify that he was dead. Even the strongest Kevlar bulletproof vests were usually only designed to withstand lower-caliber ammunition, and though its momentum would be slowed, a 7.62x32mm bullet would still have little trouble penetrating to flesh.

With the four guys down, I did a quick scan of the island and the ocean surrounding it, looking for the other half of the attack party. My heart sank in my chest as I spotted them near the center of the island, moving together in a tactical formation towards the house.

# FOURTEEN

Reaching down, I wrapped my hands around the dead guy's M4A1 at my feet. The M4 had been my go-to assault weapon during my time in the Navy, and over the years it had grown to feel more natural in my hands than a pencil. Glancing over at the four guys zeroing in on the house, I raised the M4, pressed it against my shoulder and then turned off the flashlight. I moved quickly in their direction, trying to cut the distance of about three hundred feet that stood between us.

Having heard the gunfire, they were all on high alert and looking over in my direction as I tried my best to keep behind the cover of patches of tall bushes. When it was clear that they'd spotted me, I dropped down to one knee and fired off as many rounds as I could in their direction before dropping to my chest, removing myself from their line of sight. I'd thought I'd hit at least one of them but couldn't tell as I was pinned down by a barrage of bullets buzzing just inches over the top of my head.

While taking cover, I set my M4 on the sand and reached for the frag grenade clipped to my belt. Taking a deep breath, I pulled the pin and threw a Hail Mary towards where the four guys had been clustered near the house. It exploded a second later with a loud boom, sending shards of shrapnel in all directions. The automatic gunfire stopped momentarily, and I propped myself up to get a better view. One of the guys was lying facefirst on the ground, motionless. But my eyes grew big as the three other guys opened the front door of the house and moved inside, going for Chris and his family.

My blood boiling, I jumped to my feet, threw my M4 to the ground and sprinted as fast as I could towards the house. Through the partially shattered side window, I could see the beams of their flashlights as they searched the first floor. Cutting the distance between us in a matter of seconds, I grabbed my Sig, holding it tightly in my right hand as I took one final step and pressed into the ground as hard as I could, then launched my body through the patched-up glass window. The remaining glass shattered as I crashed into the house, colliding with one of the thugs and tackling him to the hardwood floor. His head jerked back, knocking him unconscious as he dropped his AK-47 from the blow.

Raising my Sig, I put two shots into the face of one of the other thugs, causing his body to collapse to the floor in a bloody mess. Before I could shift my aim, the third guy came storming around the corner with guns blazing, his Uzi firing a stream of bullets at me. I dove behind the kitchen counter, taking cover as bullets splintered the wooden cabinets and shattered the glass. Pieces of splintered wood, cracked glasses, and shattered ceramic plates fell around me as the hail of gunfire continued. He moved in close, and as the bullets stopped, I heard his magazine fall to the floor right on the other side of the counter, signaling that he was reloading.

Jumping from my position, I fired off two shots into his bulletproof vest before he ran into me, tackling me hard into the refrigerator. Grabbing my right wrist, he slammed my hand into the counter, forcing my Sig from my grasp. As it rattled to the floor, I shoved my palm into his nose, feeling it crack to pieces, then wrapped my hand around his neck and slammed his head into the corner of the counter beside me. Blood flowed from his nose and he grunted in pain as I grabbed him by his vest and threw him to the floor. As I moved down to finish the job, he hit me with a hard kick to my abdomen, forcing me backward. He jumped to his feet as I regained my balance. Tearing open a nearby drawer, he grabbed a large knife and eyed me with hatred in his eyes and gritted, bloody teeth.

Whoever this guy was, he was strong, very strong. And he clearly had extensive hand-to-hand combat training. It also didn't help that he probably had three inches and fifty pounds of muscle on me.

Pulling open the nearest drawer to me, I glanced inside. *Shit*, I thought as I gazed upon a bunch of folded-up table linens. An instant later, the guy lunged at me. Taking a gamble, I searched under the cloth and found a lighter and a corkscrew. Grabbing the corkscrew, I gripped it in my right hand like a set of brass knuckles, the spiral metal point sticking between my middle and ring fingers. Looking up, I saw the large steel blade stabbing towards me and took a quick jump back. The blade struck hard into the cabinet, and as he ripped it loose, I kicked his face in and stabbed him twice along his right arm with the corkscrew.

The big guy yelled out in pain as he gripped the knife and swung it at my chest, blood dripping down his arm. As it sliced the air just inches away from me, I slid to the side, grabbed hold of his arm and, using his momentum against him, swung him over my body and slammed him to the floor. I heard his arm crack and reached for the loose knife on the floor as he wailed in pain. He looked me in the eyes, his face covered in blood, as I stabbed the tip of the knife down into his chest, using my body weight to cut the blade through his bulletproof vest and penetrate his heart. He gagged for a few seconds, then his eyes shut and his head dropped back against the hardwood floor.

I ripped the knife free and cleaned the bloody blade on the big guy's vest. Taking a deep breath, I wiped the sweat from my brow and stood up. Glancing in front of me, I saw a figure standing in the shadows. As he took a step towards me, I realized that it was the guy I'd tackled when I'd dived through the window. He looked dazed and had a hard time keeping his balance as he stood ten feet away from me. He held my Sig in his left hand and snarled at me as he raised it so that the barrel was pointed right at my head.

Shooting me an evil smile, he said, "Any last words, asshole?"

The silence in the living room was suddenly shattered by a loud crack. My eyes didn't blink. They stayed open and staring at the guy as a bullet exploded into his forehead and blood sprayed out the back of his skull. His body collapsed and I smelled gunpowder smoke wafting from the stairs. Turning around, I saw Cynthia standing with both feet on the third step, her arms straight out in front of her and her hands wrapped around the Beretta I'd given her earlier.

As I moved towards her, she kept the gun aimed at the dead guy and started to shake.

"Cynthia," I said, speaking as calmly as I could. My entire body was still covered in mud, so I knew that I probably looked scary as hell. "It's okay." I reached for the gun, and her eyes darted, staring into mine with a fierce gaze. "They're all dead. The island is clear for now."

She nodded softly and let out a deep sigh as she closed her eyes and loosened her grip on the Beretta enough for me to take control of it.

"I… I've never killed anybody before," she said, taking short breaths.

I wrapped my arm around her and ushered her over to the couch. After she was sitting, I told her to take deep breaths as I grabbed one of the few glasses that remained unshattered in the kitchen and filled it with water. Walking back over to her, I handed her the glass, and as she took a few sips, I moved beside her.

"Of all the people your husband could've pissed off," I said, shaking my head as I sank into the couch to catch my breath.

After a short moment of silence, I looked over at her, watching as her hands continued to shake. "Hey," I said softly, "are you alright?"

When she didn't reply, I sighed. "I know. I get it. Just remember, you only defended yourself and your family. That guy would've killed all of us if given the chance."

She shook her head back and forth a few times. “I’m not trying to justify it. I know I did the right thing.” Taking a deep breath, she let it all out and continued, “I just can’t get the image of his face out of my head.”

I sighed and rose to my feet, my back aching from being thrown into the refrigerator. I was still a little dizzy from being kicked in the face as I walked back into the kitchen, turned on the faucet and dipped my head under the water. The cold water felt good over my body, and once I’d washed my face, I took a few swigs to quench my thirst. The layer of dirt I’d rinsed off my face had pooled in the sink.

Upstairs, I heard the shuffling of feet and then the voice of one of Cynthia’s daughters calling down to make sure that we were okay. Cynthia didn’t move or even make a sound, so I walked over to her, placed my hand on her shoulder and stared sternly into her eyes.

“Your girls need you,” I said. “You have to be strong for them.”

Just as I said the words, Alex appeared on the wooden stairway. Taking one look at the two of us and the dead guys sprawled out on the floor, she ran her tiny frame over to the recliner and jumped into her mother’s lap. Burying her little face into her mother’s chest, she cried, her brown hair shaking and covering her entire head. Cynthia snapped out of it and wrapped her arms around her crying daughter.

With watery eyes, she looked up at me and said, “Tell me everything’s going to be okay. Tell me that you can protect us from all of them.”

My gaze narrowed as I stared into her sparkling brown eyes. “Everything’s going to be okay.” Then placing a hand on her daughter’s head and glanced over at the dead bodies, adding, “I can protect you from all of them.”

# FIFTEEN

I went to work hauling the bodies over to another pile under a patch of bushes, trying to hide them as best as I could. As I worked, my body aching as I dragged each corpse one by one, I thought about what I'd said to Cynthia. Deep down, I knew that there was no way of knowing whether or not I'd be able to keep my promise. For all I knew, there were fifty more guys armed just as heavily as the eight I'd just faced, waiting for the order to come and take me out. But one thing was certain—I wouldn't go down without one hell of a fight.

After hiding the final body, I looked at my dive watch and saw that it was 0230. The night sky was clear and full of stars, the ocean like glass. Having searched each corpse thoroughly, I added a few toys to my arsenal, including two more M26 frag grenades, an incendiary grenade, an M4A1 with three spare magazines, and a Kevlar bulletproof vest, which I donned right away. I threw all my weapons into the chest in the kitchen pantry except my Sig, which I holstered to my leg, the M4, which I kept slung over my shoulder, and two grenades, which I kept clipped onto my belt. I also had an extra magazine for both my Sig and my M4 strapped around my waist, ready to be withdrawn at a moment's notice if need be. The last thing I wanted was to be caught off guard while moving about the island with nothing but my Sig and dive knife at my side.

I headed back up the long spiral staircase and spent a few minutes looking out over the horizon in all directions. The salvage vessel was still anchored in the same spot, about a half of a mile off the northern tip of the island. But aside from it, there were no other boats on the water. Staring at the old rusted ship through the lens of my night vision monocular, I watched as a handful of guys scattered about on the deck. Dropping the monocular to my side, I took in a deep breath. I had no way of knowing how many of them were on the ship, but there was one thing I did know. When they decided to come back to Loggerhead, they'd do it with a much larger force than they had before. I'd dealt with assholes like Salazar many times over the course of my life, and they all had one thing in common: they hated to lose.

I reached for the small radio that was still resting at the foot of my blue folding chair. Flipping it on, I did a quick scan of the channels, and when I couldn't get a signal, I switched it back off. The battery was getting dangerously low, its mini digital display illuminating just one red bar, and I couldn't find a spare battery anywhere.

Grabbing my thermos from the floor, I took a few swigs of the lukewarm coffee, then set it back down. Looking out at the ship, I decided that if I was going to fight off another attack, I would need to be more prepared. In the basement of the lighthouse, I found an old fishing tackle box filled with lures, bobbers and two coils of fishing line. Thinking back to a raid I'd been on back in Colombia, where the local rebels had used booby traps to try and hold us back, I got an idea.

Snatching the fishing line, I headed out the door and set up three snares, using the coconut trees surrounding the old white house and the lighthouse to hold them in place. I wrapped the twenty-five-pound test lines around the trunks of the trees, then, with tension in the lines, tied each end off to one of the grenades, tying one knot to the body and the other knot to the detonation pin. Then, very carefully, I covered the grenades with a few small branches and leaves that had fallen in the storm, concealing them from view. The M26 frag grenade has an injury radius of about fifty feet and a lethal radius of fifteen feet, and since I'd placed them in between palms that were about a hundred feet apart, no matter where these thugs tripped the line, they'd at least get injured. The three booby traps created a perimeter that almost circled the entire center of the island, leaving just a few narrow passages between them.

As I was setting up the traps, I noticed something odd about part of the landscape about three hundred feet southwest of the southernmost coconut trees. Moving over to a small pile of white sand that looked unnatural, I dug into the sand with my hands for a few minutes and soon found that there was something hard buried about a foot down. The storm must have covered it, I thought, as I continued to dig, soon realizing that it was a large rectangular sheet of mahogany about five feet wide and seven feet long.

Digging my fingers underneath its edges, I grunted and lifted it up, revealing a small storage space underneath it. There was nothing useful inside, just a few empty wooden crates and some shovels and plastic rakes, but it would be a good hiding place if I ever needed to move the Hales. Dropping the board back down, I covered it with a few inches of sand, then headed over to the old white house.

After taking a quick trip upstairs to warn the others to stay inside and not stray from the house, I moved to the back of the house and examined the propane tank beside the broken back window. It looked to be a five-hundred-gallon tank, which I verified by reading the data plate under the aluminum lid. Beside the data plate was a gauge that read about seventy-two percent, meaning that there was right around 360 gallons of propane in the tank.

With no explosives on the island other than the grenades, I knew I'd have to make do. Following the black line out of the top of the tank, I saw that it split off, with one hose heading to the main house and the other straying off towards the lighthouse. Kneeling down, I shut the isolation valve for the lighthouse line, making it so all the propane would be directed towards the main house. Following the line inside the house, I found where it connected to both the heaters and the kitchen stove and burned their locations into my mind.

My night vision monocular in hand, I headed back outside and, avoiding my booby traps, walked towards the northeast beach, where the second group of four thugs had landed on the island. Looking out over the horizon, I could see the dark outline of the ship in the distance. Down on the beach, the scrape marks left by their boat were still visible in the sand just up from the surf.

Suddenly, my body froze as I heard a bullet zip past my ear and bury itself in the ground behind me, spraying up a pile of sand in its wake. A split second later, I heard the report of a large-caliber rifle and hurled my body, diving flat onto my stomach behind a small sandbank. Two more bullets followed immediately after the first, hitting the pile of sand in front of me. I listened intently as the cracking of gunpowder echoed from far out to sea. Someone had a sniper rifle on that ship, I thought as I lay with my head buried in the sand. Fortunately for me, though, the guy pulling the trigger wasn't a crack shot. Crawling backwards away from the beach, I moved into the cover of thick shrubs and headed slowly back towards the center of the island.

When I'd moved far enough away from the beach, I stood up and tried to zoom in and spot the guy using my monocular. But the ship was too far away. All I could do was shake my head, wishing I had a weapon with the range and scope to take him out.

As I headed back towards the lighthouse, Cynthia was standing by the door. She was staring at me with wide eyes that glistened by the light of the silver moon overhead.

"What happened?" she asked, her voice filled with worry. "We all heard the gunshots."

I shook my head. "A close call, that's what happened." Moving closer to her, I added, "Seriously, no straying beyond the house and lighthouse, alright?" She nodded, and I continued, "These guys are gonna come after us with their full force soon. They have to. Now that Fay has passed, these waters will soon come to life with fishing boats and Coast

Guard patrols. They must know that they're running out of time."

She stared at me with the stone-cold expression of a worried-to-death mother. I wasn't trying to scare her. I just wanted them to be ready for what was about to happen.

"How many more do you think that they have?" she asked.

I shrugged. "I don't know. I'd bet at least twenty, though." Looking out in the direction of the ship, I said, "I need you all to be ready and do exactly as I say, alright?" Then, looking at her waist, I saw that she was carrying her Beretta in a black holster. Half of the weapon was covered by the bottom of her dirty black tank top.

She glanced down at it, then back up at me. "I took it from one of the dead guys."

I smiled and, feeling the fatigue of the day start to sink in a little, I said, "Any chance I could get some more of that coffee? My thermos is cold and running a little dry."

"It's filled to the brim now," she said with a smile. "I figured you'd be running low."

I thanked her and told her again to be ready for anything before opening the door to the lighthouse and heading up the long spiral staircase.

# SIXTEEN

At 0500, the first hints of sunlight radiated over the eastern sky, sending a faint red-and-yellow glow in all directions. For the past few hours, there had been little to no activity aboard the distant ship. A few guys walking about, patrolling the decks or staring at the island through their scopes, but nothing more.

But in the last ten minutes or so, more and more guys had filled the decks, shuffling about as orders were yelled at them from a few guys standing on the control platform at the top of the vessel. Clearly, they were planning something, but there was no way of knowing how or when they would strike.

The odds were stacked heavily against me. If they stormed the beach utilizing all three skiffs, they'd be able to come at us from all directions. Three booby traps and an exploding propane tank could only do so much against a trained and well-equipped army.

Reaching for the small old radio at my feet, I

made one final desperate attempt to send a message out to anyone nearby who could help us. As I scanned through the channels, I heard nothing but static as the single red bar indicating what remained of the battery started to blink. When I reached channel sixteen, I held the button and spoke into the microphone.

"This is an SOS. I repeat, SOS. This is Logan Dodge. I'm stranded on Loggerhead Key, along with four others, and in immediate need of assistance."

I waited for a second and then my eyes grew wide. My jaw practically dropped to the floor as I heard a voice struggle its way through the radio static.

"This is Coast Guard Rescue six-zero-four-seven. Logan.... We're... Loggerhead..."

The guy's words broke in and out of clarity as the terrible signal crackled over his voice. It was a Coast Guard Jayhawk helicopter and, judging from the bits and pieces of words that had made it unscathed to my ears, they sounded like they were heading in our direction. Holding down the talk button, I spoke as loudly and clearly as I could into the microphone, warning the pilots that the island was surrounded by heavily armed Cuban gangsters. But before I could receive a reply other than the loud, annoying static, the radio went silent and its LED screen turned dark.

My heart raced as I stared at the useless hunk of plastic in my hands. I was glad that I'd finally been able to get word out about our situation but equally pissed off by the fact that the Coast Guard rescue crew, who were in all likelihood heading in our direction at that very moment, had no idea what they were flying themselves into. Sure, there was a small chance they'd be able to land near the lighthouse, load all five of us up, then take off and fly away unscathed. But that wasn't likely. Especially with that sniper on the salvage ship holding down the beach. The possibility of bullets damaging the helicopter or injuring one of their crewmembers was real, and it was a thought I couldn't clear out of my mind.

Grabbing my binoculars, I did a quick survey of the dimly lit horizon in all directions. Seeing no sign of the helicopter, and seeing that all three skiffs were still strapped to the deck of the ship, I headed down the stairs and over to the nearby house. As I rushed my strides, I tried with all my strength to imagine an outcome where we all made it out of there alive and well, but it was really hard to do. The inside of the house was quiet and my footsteps creaked the old wooden steps as I made my way up to the second floor and into the bedroom. The four of them were all asleep on the queen-sized bed as I entered, bundled together beneath a seashell-patterned quilt. The young girls huddled over their parents as they leaned back against two old pillows covered in pillowcases that looked like they should have been trashed long ago.

As the bedroom door hit the wall with a bang, Chris and Cynthia both opened their eyes in unison and looked frantically in my direction as they both sat up.

"What's going on?" Chris asked as his two daughters rolled slowly out of bed.

I told them that, after receiving a signal on the radio, I'd spoken to a Coast Guard helicopter pilot and that they might be on their way to the island.

Cynthia stared at me, her hazel eyes showing a faint glimmer of hope.

"When?" she asked, removing the covers and stepping out of the bed fully dressed.

I shook my head. "I don't know. The radio died

only seconds after we started talking to each other. But since I was able to reach them with that short-range radio, I'm guessing they're nearby. Probably looking for stragglers like us who got caught up in the storm."

Chris shifted onto the edge of the bed, staring at the wooden floor near his feet. He still looked like hell from when those guys had beat him up, and his right leg was wrapped up in bandages.

"What do we do?" he asked gravely.

"We get ready," I said. "We have to be prepared for if the Coast Guard does arrive, but whether they do or don't show up, those thugs out on that ship are up to something. And I promise you this, they sure as hell aren't just gonna sit by and watch as a helicopter flies us all out of here."

Cynthia grabbed her holster from the nightstand, strapped it around her waist and locked in the Beretta. As the four of them moved towards me, Cynthia looked me over from head to toe and said, "You still haven't slept, have you?"

I didn't answer her. Thinking about how I hadn't slept in over twenty-four hours would only make it worse, and I could already feel the fatigue starting to take over.

As I helped Chris down the stairs and lowered him onto a wooden chair beside the front door, I heard a distant humming sound coming from outside. Opening the door, I stepped out onto the small run-down porch and listened intently as the humming sound grew louder and louder. It was unmistakable, a sound I'd heard countless times before in my life. The sound of helicopter blades slicing through the air at high speeds.

I stepped down onto the beach and looked out

over the eastern horizon, the direction the sounds were coming from. The sun had risen just enough at my back to illuminate the morning sky, allowing me to see a shadowy object flying a few thousand feet over the ocean, heading straight for our island.

"What is it?" Cynthia asked as she stepped through the door. But before she'd reached the end of the porch, her eyes lit up and she glanced over at me. "Logan, it's them."

I nodded but knew that we were still far from being home free. As I brushed past her, I said, "Make sure everyone's ready to move with a purpose when that thing touches down."

Heading back inside, I walked past Chris, who was sitting beside the door, his daughters standing beside him.

"What's going on?" he said as I moved towards the pantry. I opened it up and pulled out the old chest, which was now filled to the brim with the weapons from all of the men I'd taken down. "That sure sounds like a helicopter to me."

Opening the chest, I dug through the pile of weapons and pulled out a flare gun I'd found in the lighthouse. "It's the Coast Guard," I said, watching as the two girls lit up, their faces contorting into smiles for the first time since they'd arrived on the island.

Chris's mouth practically fell to the old hardwood floor below. His eyes grew wide. "Logan, that means—"

"It means that we're not out of this yet," I said, cutting him off as I loaded up the flare gun and headed back towards the front door.

I almost walked right into Cynthia as she stormed back inside. "It's getting close," she said, unable to contain the excitement in her voice.

Before heading outside to signal the helicopter, I wrapped my arms around the four of them, forming a small huddle. "Look," I said, my eyes scanning each of them, trying to convey to them the seriousness of the situation we were in. "I'm gonna signal them to land just outside the house here. You guys stay inside and be ready to move when I say so. Nobody takes so much as a step out of this door until I give the all clear, understand?" I waited until each of them spoke up, letting me know that they understood, then continued, "Just hold tight and be ready to run. I'll come over to help with you." I pointed at Chris.

With the sounds of the helicopter growing louder in the distance, I headed out the front door, shutting it snug behind me, then raced over to a large clearing between the old white house and the lighthouse. It was more than big enough to allow for the helicopter to land, and it was far away from any of the booby traps I'd set the night before. Standing in the middle, I raised up the flare gun, pointing it into the dim morning sky, then pulled the trigger when the helicopter was less than a mile away from the island. The flare exploded from the barrel, hissing high into the sky and glowing bright red, leaving a thin trail of white smoke behind it.

Throwing the flare gun to the ground, I ran around the lighthouse and watched as the helicopter made its approach to the island and started to descend. As I'd expected from their call sign, it was an MH-60T Jayhawk, painted in the distinct white and orange of the Coast Guard. The sounds of its spinning rotors shook the quiet air as it flew right over my position at an altitude of about a thousand feet. After passing over the island, it made a wide turn south, hovering over the entirety of the island before slowing back towards the large clearing where I'd fired the flare.

I waved my hands wildly to get their attention as they kept the bird in place for a few moments. Wondering what the hell they were waiting for, I focused on them through my monocular and saw that one of the guys was staring and pointing a gloved finger at something out in the ocean. Turning around, I scanned the horizon and my heart sank deep into my chest. I saw a boat full of thugs cruising just a few hundred feet from the shoreline, their heads swiveled and their eyes staring at the chopper.

Every instinct in my body told me to grab the M4 slung to my back, run closer to the beach and send a deadly wave of bullets in their direction. I took a few steps towards the beach as their boat turned sharply, heading straight for the eastern beach. The helicopter was still hovering about a thousand feet above, its rotors blocking out all other sounds and sending a swirl of strong winds all around me. I knew that if I did grab my M4 and open fire, the Coast Guard guys might suspect that I was the bad one and put me right in the crosshairs of their M240 machine gun.

I waited for a moment, wondering what both the helicopter and the thugs in the boat were going to do next. To my surprise, the gangsters hadn't opened fire on the helicopter. In fact, as I focused my gaze on their boat, I realized that none of the guys were even holding guns. I shook my head, unable to comprehend what they were up to. As I waited for the helicopter pilots to make up their minds, I grabbed my monocular to get a better look at the men on the skiff. They were still watching the helicopter intently as their boat motored closer and closer to the shore. I wondered for a brief moment if they'd planned to jump onto the beach and do a surprise attack just as the helicopter was landing and the five of us were out in the open. Then, I saw the tip of a distinct object in one of the thug's hands. He tried to keep it hidden beneath the side of the hull but had let it rise up just long enough for me to realize exactly what it was—a rocket-propelled grenade launcher.

"Holy shit," I said to myself as the helicopter started to drop in altitude, clearly deciding to land on the patch of grass right behind where I was standing. I tried to wave them off, to somehow communicate that it wasn't safe to land, but it was no use. From their angle, right on top of me, it was impossible for them to even see me, let alone comprehend what I was trying to tell them. Looking back towards the thugs, I grabbed my M4 and took aim, knowing that I had no other choice but to take them out.

With the helicopter roaring down behind me, blowing a strong breeze against my back, I placed my finger on the trigger and held it down firmly, sending a barrage of automatic gunfire straight at the boat. I hit a few of them, sending a bullet through a guy's face and two more through another guy's chest before they realized what was happening and took cover, dropping to the deck and out of my view. I continued to fire, rattling round after round into the fiberglass hull while moving closer to their position. In the back of my mind, I thought about the sniper who'd shot at me from the ship the previous night. This forced me to stick to the shrubs a few hundred feet from the beach, keeping myself out of the ship's line of sight.

As the boat started to turn and cruise parallel with the shore, I drew my fire towards the engine, causing it to spit out clouds of black smoke. A few thugs held their weapons over the side of the hull, trying their best to at least shoot in my general direction, but it was no use. I had them pinned down and they knew it. Dropping the empty magazine to the dirt, I reached for my spare and had it jammed up into the bottom of the rifle in less than half of a second.

The helicopter pilot, after seeing the events taking place on the beach, quickly changed course and tried to regain their lost elevation as fast as he could. I took aim once more, firing more rounds into the helpless boat as its momentum stopped and its pontoons deflated offshore, dead in the water.

As I heard the helicopter start to veer away from me overhead, a bright ball of fire flashed from inside the boat, followed instantly by the sound of a powerful explosion. My eyes grew big and my heart stopped as I watched a rocket launch from the boat and hiss loudly through the air towards the helicopter. As the chopper started to turn, the rocket screamed, exploding into its tail in a bright yellow fireball.

# SEVENTEEN

The explosion shook the ground and echoed like thunder through the air. The tail end of the helicopter had been almost completely blown to pieces. All that remained was deformed shards of burning metal as the rear rotor fell from the sky, crashing into the sand in a scorched mess less than a hundred feet away from me. The helicopter lost all control as it jerked wildly across the sky, picking up speed as it spiraled helplessly down towards the ground below.

I watched as the pilot tried to stabilize the helicopter, but after losing the tail rotor and most of the tail along with it, it was clear that he was in a losing battle. The engines roared angrily as the flames continued to burn, spreading dangerously close to the fuel tank. Plumes of black smoke radiated from the dying craft in all directions as it fell below a thousand feet, spinning wildly and rocketing towards the beach like a meteor.

I took cover and could only watch as the

damaged helicopter screamed through the air over my head, then crashed into the ocean just a few hundred feet from the shore, sending a chaotic fountain of water bursting into the air. The white sand shook beneath my feet, and pieces of metal and shattered glass flew out in all directions as the helicopter tumbled ferociously through the water, its main rotor blade spraying sheets of seawater for a split second before being ripped free from the motor.

The hot, roaring flames from the metal fire continued to burn as what remained of the helicopter came to a stop halfway beneath the waves. I felt a surge of anger deep inside as I ran as fast as I could towards the beach. The thugs' boat floated helplessly in the water, but I could see a few heads poking up and the barrels of their weapons as they stared at the burning wreckage. Turning over my left shoulder, I realized that fortunately the ship was out of view, just hidden around the northern portion of the island. Grabbing my M4, I fired off a spray of bullets, blowing two of their heads into a bloody heap as they fell from view.

Splashing through the shallows, I came to the boat, which was floating in just a few feet of water. Only one of the four guys on board was alive, and just as I peeked over the side of the hull, I saw him reach for an AK-47 lying on the deck beside him. Diving over the transom, I tackled his crawling body, slamming it to the fiberglass deck as I reached for my dive knife. Without hesitation, I stabbed the blade into the back of his neck, piercing his skull. Sliding my blade free, I wiped the blood off, then secured it to my leg again.

With my heart racing like a freight train, I jumped back into the water and sprinted towards the burning wreck that only moments earlier had been a functioning Jayhawk helicopter. The water quickly rose up past my waist, forcing me to dive headfirst and swim freestyle as fast as I could through the warm Caribbean water. I could feel the heat from the burning rubble as I reached the helicopter, which was propped up on its side against a shallow reef. Looking through the shattered windows, I saw that most of the cockpit was filled with water. Careful to avoid the rows of glass shards, I crawled inside.

The two pilots were bloody and not moving. I did a quick check of their vitals, but it was clear that they were dead. Pulling my body into the cabin, I saw a third guy leaning against the top of the helicopter, his body shaking as he held his hands pressed against his chest. Thick splotches of blood oozed through his orange rescue suit. He was still wearing his helmet and face shield, allowing me to just barely see his eyes as he glanced up at me.

Splashing my body through the few feet of water inside the craft, I did a quick assessment of his injuries and, realizing how bad they were, decided I had to get him out of the helicopter as quickly and as carefully as possible. I would have tried to help him right there, but with the fire still burning what remained of the tail, I knew that the fuel tank could explode at any moment, killing us both in an explosion of flames.

"I'm gonna get you out of here," I said, staring into his eyes. He'd already lost a good amount of blood, and judging by the way his body was shaking, I estimated I had no more than a few minutes to try and save him.

I wrapped my arm around his upper body, trying to rotate him around so I could pull him out. But before I could get a good hold on him, he squeezed my shirt tightly with his left hand.

"No," he said suddenly, closing his eyes and wincing in pain. "Leave me be, Logan." His words struggled from his mouth as his intense eyes focused mine.

I heard a slight familiarity in his voice, and by the way he said my name, it seemed as though he knew me.

"I'm getting you out of here," I said, staring into his eyes and letting him know that I wasn't about to let him die without doing everything I could to help him.

He lifted his gloved hand slightly, trying to wave me off. "I'm already done for," he said, coughing and squinting as blood continued to flow out between the fingers pressed against his chest. "Can you take this off?" he said, motioning to the helmet and face shield covering his entire head.

Carefully, I unclipped the plastic strap, tucked my hands under the sides and slowly lifted it up. My eyes grew wide as I recognized the dying young man in front of me. My mind raced back to a few days earlier, when I'd met him while hunting pythons with Jack in the Everglades. His short brown hair and his lean young face were unmistakable.

"I need you to do something for me," Ryan said, his dark eyes filling with salty tears as he struggled to get his final words out. "I need you to tell my wife that I love her." His body shook as he gagged for air, willing himself to continue. "And my son, Logan." He tilted his head back and his eyes shut slowly. "Look after him for me."

He took one final, painstaking breath, and then his body went limp. I wiped the tears from my eyes, then placed my hand on his forehead and told him that I would do as he'd asked.

A loud roar of flames and the sound of creaking metal snatched me out of the moment, reminding me that the wrecked helicopter I was standing inside was on fire and could blow sky-high any second. Taking one more look at the dead young man, I moved to the front of the chopper and crawled over the shards of shattered glass, splashing into the water on the other side. There had been a few moments in my life where I'd seen things, images that I'd never been able to clear from my mind. As I swam for the shore, I knew that seeing Ryan lying dead in the back of that wrecked helicopter would be one of them.

When I reached the surface, I dug my feet into the sand and trudged through the water, reaching the sandy beach in less than a minute. Standing on the shore for a moment, I turned around and watched as the flames continued to spread throughout the crashed, partially sunken helicopter. Within a few seconds of my arriving on the beach, the flames reached the fuel tank and what remained of the chopper was blown to pieces in a massive ball of fire. The explosion shook the ground and was so loud that I was sure anyone within a hundred-mile radius of the island must have heard it.

I gritted my teeth as I watched the helicopter burn, shooting a massive plume of black smoke high into the air. My heart raced, the adrenaline pumping blood through my veins at a dangerous rate. I narrowed my gaze and clenched my fists. Those assholes were going to pay for this. I was going to bring each and every one of them down, or I was going to die trying.

Looking down the beach, I watched as the

deflated boat floated aimlessly passed the southern tip of Loggerhead, its useless engine still shooting plumes of black smoke and its hull riddled to pieces with bullet holes. A few dead guys lay sprawled out over the sides, blood dripping from their bodies into the ocean below. The clear morning sky was lit up in an array of reds and pinks, making it easy to see without the need for my night vision monocular.

Grabbing my M4 from where I'd thrown it on the beach, I brushed off the sand and moved swiftly back toward the center of the island. As I thought about how I was going to engage the ship, knowing that they still had two more boats, a helicopter and who knew how many more men, I heard the sounds of two outboard engines echoing across the water, coming from the direction of the ship. It appeared as though the thugs had finally had enough and were coming to hunt me down with their full force and finish the job. Gripping my M4, I couldn't help but smile as they motored closer to the island. Salazar and his gang had messed with the wrong guy.

# EIGHTEEN

"Follow me," I said, standing in the door frame of the old white house after creaking the front door open. As I stepped towards the wooden chair by the door I helped Chris to his feet.

"Where are we going?" he asked sternly.

"We heard explosions," Cynthia added, her voice filled with worry and dejection.

"There isn't time to explain," I said, ushering them towards the door as I supported most of Chris's weight with my right arm.

As I led the four of them down the old wooden steps, I heard the sounds of the boats moving closer, heading around the northern tip towards the eastern side of the island. Moving away from the house, I led them through a gap of about five feet between two coconut trees, making sure that they each avoided the clear fishing line tensioned out on both sides. The last thing I wanted was for one of my booby traps to be used against us. Moving as fast as we could, we maneuvered around thick green bushes and over small sand dunes for about a minute before reaching our destination.

Making sure Cynthia had Chris's weight supported, I bent down, pushed aside a few inches of loose sand and dug my fingers under the sheet of mahogany I'd found earlier. When I had a good grip, I pulled it up, sending sand cascading over the sides as I revealed the small hollowed-out space below. It looked like it hadn't been used or taken care of much over the years, but it would do the job of hiding the family.

Looking at the four of them, I motioned my head towards the space. "Get inside."

They hesitated a moment, then, seeing the ferocity in my eyes, Cynthia crawled inside and held up her hands to help her two daughters.

"Keep quiet," I said as I helped Chris down, then did a quick scan of the beach to make sure that none of the thugs were nearby, watching where I was hiding the four of them.

"What happened?" Cynthia asked, staring gravely over the eastern side of the island at the thick trail of black smoke rising high into the air.

I waved her off. "Just stay here and keep quiet. When I come back, I'll stomp three times, so you know that it's me." Then I looked off into the distance, took in a deep breath of fresh air and added, "Look, if something happens to me, your only hope is to stay hidden here. That smoke can be seen for miles. Now that the storm has passed, it's only a matter of hours until more help arrives on the island. But if these guys do find you, you know what to do." I nodded at the Beretta strapped to her hip.

As I lowered the sheet of mahogany, I saw that

Jordan and Alex were starting to cry and had wrapped their arms around their parents. Over the past twenty-four hours, I'd tried my best to avoid talking about the situation with them close by, not wanting to frighten them any more than they already were. But I had no other choice at that moment.

"Be careful," Cynthia said as she crouched down, staring up at me with her family huddled beside her as I lowered the sheet back down onto the sand.

I didn't reply. The truth was, I had no intention of being careful. Salazar and his goons had pissed me off more than I could describe, and for the first time in years, I was gonna let myself go wild. I would give in to my adrenaline-fueled body and hold nothing back.

I spent a few brief moments hiding the wooden sheet as best as I could, shoving piles of sand over the top of it and smoothing it out so it blended with the area around it. Grabbing a few fallen palm leaves, I set them on top, then turned on my heels and headed back towards the house. It didn't look perfect by any means, but it was the best I could do with the short amount of time I had.

Just as I reached the side of the house, the sounds of the outboards suddenly went silent, one right after the other, signaling that both boats had landed on the beach. Kneeling down, I lifted the green plastic lid and opened the isolation valve to the propane tank, allowing it to pressurize the hose leading into the house, then shut the lid and moved inside through the front door. Once inside, I ran upstairs, then propped the bedroom window fully open using a small length of two-by-four set aside for that purpose and pushed aside the old curtains. Then I rushed back downstairs into the kitchen and opened the cabinet next to the stove. Using my dive knife, I crawled inside and cut the black rubber line leading to the propane tank outside, letting the highly explosive gas flow freely into the house.

As I stood up, I pulled open a kitchen drawer and grabbed one of the tablecloths, along with the lighter I'd seen the previous night while fighting the big thug. I wrapped them both in a few layers of Saran wrap, then shoved them into the front pocket of my wet cargo shorts. Opening the pantry, I knelt down and pried open the old chest. As fast as I could, I grabbed what I needed, including an extra M4 magazine, a sawed-off shotgun, the two remaining grenades and my spear gun along with two spears. Shoving it all into the large roller bag stashed beside the chest, I moved swiftly across the living room and through the front door, the faint sound of leaking gas hissing in the air. Slamming it shut behind me, I stood on the porch for a moment and did a quick scan of the area around me. With the roller bag resting on the porch, I held my M4 with a tight grip as I looked for any nearby bad guys, ready to fire at a moment's notice. When I saw that it was clear, I sprinted for the lighthouse.

Opening the door, I took one more glance towards the surf and spotted a few thugs, their heads barely visible over the thick shrubs along the top of a sandbank. I heard the loud barking of orders as they moved in my direction, but before they spotted me, I stepped into the lighthouse and shut the door behind me, sliding the small piece of brass sideways, locking the door. Striding across the dimly lit room, I set the roller bag on the floor, grabbed the edges of a large cherry bookcase filled with volumes and threw it forward, slamming it onto the ground. Leaning forward, I pushed it, scraping the floor as I forced it up against the door. I piled a few more items on top of it, including a table and chairs, then headed upstairs. I knew that it wouldn't keep them from getting inside, but it would sure as hell slow them down.

Halfway up the tall spiral staircase, I froze as I heard an explosion resonate with a muffled boom through the brick walls. It had sounded like a grenade, indicating that one of my booby traps had been tripped. When I reached the top of the stairs, I looked down through the glass windows and saw one man on the ground, his body bloody and covered with shrapnel that stuck deep into his skin. A few more guys limped, clearly wounded by the grenade as they struggled towards the house. A few of the thugs yelled out orders, and the large group closed in on the old house, going after the family just as I'd thought they would.

With that guy down, I counted fifteen still on their feet, most of them as heavily armed as the professionals I'd taken out earlier that morning. All but three wore bulletproof vests, and most of them wore plated helmets. Staring down at them through the window, I watched as they surrounded the house like a SWAT team preparing to make a major drug bust. Four of the thugs approached the front door, covered from behind and at their flanks by the others.

As they reached for the doorknob I knelt down, reached inside the large roller bag, and pulled out my spear gun and one metal spear. Digging into my wet pocket, I pulled out the tablecloth and the lighter I'd covered in Saran wrap to keep from getting soaked. Sliding my dive knife from its sheath, I tore off a piece of the tablecloth, then tied it around the tip of the spear. I made sure to use only as much cloth as I needed, not wanting to weigh down the spear too much or throw off its aerodynamics any more than was necessary. Then, using the pointed tip of my knife, I poked a crack in the Bic lighter and held it over the tied piece of tablecloth, pouring the lighter fluid out and soaking the cloth in highly flammable liquid. Loading the spear onto the gun track, I pulled back on the two elastic bands and locked it into place.

When I looked back down through the glass, the four men had already entered through the wide open front door, followed closely behind by two more. That was my chance. It had been long enough since I'd cut the hose that most if not all of the 360 gallons of propane would have depressurized from the tank, changed phase to a gas, and filled the empty house. Grabbing my spear gun in one hand and the lighter in the other, I held the top of the lighter up close to the tip of the spear and flicked it a couple of times. Sparks shot out, a few of them landing on the fluid-soaked tablecloth and causing it to go up in flames.

Dropping the lighter, I held my spear gun shoulder height, then unlatched the window facing the house and pushed it open. Moving one step outside, I took aim at the middle of the open upstairs window, then squeezed the trigger. The stretched bands snapped free, launching the spear through the air towards the house at over one hundred and fifty feet per second. It shot straight through the open window, and in an instant, the flaming tip ignited the propane-filled house, turning the entire structure into one giant bomb. The massive explosion boomed as balls of fire shot out from the house. The flames spread instantaneously, engulfing the entire house in flames as half of the roof was blown high into the air. Pieces of torched, splintered wood flew out in all directions as a large plume of smoke mushroomed up into the morning sky.

# NINETEEN

There was no chance for the six men who'd gone inside. They were charred alive instantly as they were surrounded by the ignited flammable gas. Two of the guys who'd stood by aimlessly providing cover from the side of the house were on fire and rolled frantically in the shrubs, trying to put themselves out. Grabbing my M4, I took aim and put each of them out of their misery with clean shots through their skulls. Once they were dead, I turned my aim towards one of the other guys on the ground but was forced to drop for cover as bullets shattered the glass and deflected around the tiny room. One of the bullets exploded through the rotating light, destroying the bulb and extinguishing its beam from the sky around the island.

As the bullets continued to fly into the small space from all directions below, I thought about the thugs who'd been killed already. There were still seven down there, alive and kicking, and that was assuming no more bad guys had shown up from the ship. I heard a guy yell, and then the firing stopped abruptly so I popped my head up, taking a look at the damage. The entire wraparound window was shattered, leaving only a few pointy shards around the edges. I hoisted myself for a better view of the ground and saw that they'd moved towards the door to the lighthouse.

Jumping to my feet, I grabbed one of the grenades and clipped it to my belt. Then, I switched my M4 out for the sawed-off shotgun, which would be more effective in the close quarters of the stairwell, and pocketed a handful of shells. Turning around, I ran down the stairs that seemed to never end, spiraling around over and over before finally reaching the bottom. When I did, I saw that the thugs had already made good progress on my makeshift barricade. They were slamming their bodies against the door as I kept to the shadows of the room, thinking of a plan. When they'd forced the door about halfway open, causing a stream of morning light to illuminate the dark room, I reached for the grenade clipped to my belt.

Pulling the pin, I held down the safety lever, reared it back and lobbed it through the partially open door. The guys on the other side were caught off guard by the sight of it. They yelled out curses and dove for cover as the grenade exploded, sending a pile of sharpened pieces of shrapnel darting through the air in all directions. They screamed in pain following the loud blast, and I heard at least one body collapse to the ground just outside the door. I heard them scramble, and just moments after the blast, they were firing their automatic weapons at the door. I moved up a few stairs and dropped down for cover as hundreds of bullets shattered the door, splintering it to pieces along with the bookcase, table, and chairs that were propped behind it. I felt like I was in a war zone as their bullets screamed through the air, rattling against the walls of the room.

After about five seconds of solid fire, from what sounded like at least three rifles, the shooting stopped. In the relative silence that followed, one of the guys yelled out for them to move in. Just as I saw the first guy appear in the doorway, I turned around and moved quietly back upstairs. Stopping halfway up, I moved into the small storage space where I'd found the blue folding chair and hid in the shadows behind an old wooden crate. Listening, I heard them talking amongst themselves in the room below, followed soon after by the sounds of their boots stomping their way up the stairs straight for me.

I cracked open my sawed-off shotgun, verifying again that there were shells inserted, then shut it back up. As the first thug ran by me, I grabbed my dive knife with my left hand, sprang from my position and stabbed down into the base of his neck. Blood splattered out as he gagged, and holding the sawed-off shotgun tightly with my right hand, I aimed it around the dying thug and blasted a storm of lead pellets into the second guy's head. His face was torn apart in a mess of blood as his body fell backward, the sound of the shell exploding deafening in the tight space of the stairwell.

Before I could take aim at the third guy as he appeared around the corner, he pulled the trigger on his MAC-10 Uzi, firing a stream of bullets straight towards me. Two of the bullets caught me, driving into the left side of my bulletproof vest and causing me to grunt in pain, feeling as though I'd just been hit twice with a sledgehammer. Using the two dead guys as cover, I tackled them down the stairs, hurtling our bodies towards the third guy as he continued to fire off round after round. Aiming forward, I blasted the second shell from my shotgun into the third thug's chest, shredding the skin from his hands. He yelled wildly as he dropped his Uzi. The three of us plowed into him, and we tumbled violently down the stairs, my body slamming into flailing limbs and the pointed angles of the stairs. It hurt like hell as we rounded the corner, slamming into a fourth guy who was standing in the middle and jumped sideways to try and avoid us but couldn't.

He stepped backward, almost losing his balance as the four of us slowed to a painful stop. I felt like hell. Pain surged from every corner of my body as I struggled to my feet, still gripping my dive knife tightly in my left hand. Just as I looked up, the fourth guy, who was much bigger and stronger than the other guys, slammed his meaty fist across the side of my face. My head snapped sideways, and blood sprayed out of my mouth. It felt like he'd broken half of the muscles in my face as I turned back to engage him. I was met with a strong front kick, his massive boot hitting me square in the chest like a freight train and knocking all the air from my lungs. I fell backward, landing on top of the three sprawled-out bodies behind me.

As I looked up, rage coursing through my veins, I saw the barrel of the big thug's revolver aiming straight at my head. It was hard to tell on the stairs, but he looked to be at least six foot five and probably weighed two hundred and fifty pounds. He had dark tanned skin and black hair cut close to his scalp. His black eyes glared at me, and a vein stuck out from his forehead as his face contorted, revealing his anger.

"Where are they?" he snarled, pulling back the hammer of his revolver and moving the end of the barrel within a few inches of my face.

I took a few quick breaths, assessing the situation for a moment before replying. My mind was dazed from the blow, and I pictured the image of Ryan's dying body in the back of the helicopter. I spat out a spray of blood, the red gobs splattering across his gray cutoff shirt, which was stretched so tight from his bulging muscles that it looked like it would tear at any moment.

Staring deep into his menacing eyes, I said, "You'll never get them."

His eyes grew wide, and he growled violently as he wiped a few red splotches from his face. "Where are they?" he yelled, bringing his revolver sideways and slamming the handle towards my forehead.

I forced my head back in an instant, the handle soaring less than an inch from my forehead as I squeezed my hands around his massive wrist and jammed the gun into the brick wall beside us. The revolver fell from his grasp, clattering down the wooden steps beneath us. Still digging my hands into his right wrist, I punched him square in the nose, feeling the fragile bones crack under my knuckles. His massive head jerked backward as blood flowed down over his mouth. I tried to stand up, but before I could, his bulky hands were wrapped around my neck, his fingers squeezing the life out of me. He growled, and I felt my windpipe start to crack as he squeezed even harder, his eyes bulging out of his blood-splattered face.

As the world around me started to fade, I jerked my chin into my chest, then bit down on his left thumb, feeling it crack like a carrot between my teeth.

He yelled out viciously and loosened his grip just enough for me to force his hands off me. Gasping for a quick breath, I dug my heels into his massive chest and straightened my legs with all of my strength, kicking his body backward. The oversized thug slammed onto his back, tumbling down the stairs with one loud crash after another. I distinctly heard more than one major bone crack before he finally slowed to a stop around the corner and out of my view.

My body still hurt like hell from my own roll down the stairs as I rose to my feet. My jaw felt funny, and the right side of my face screamed in pain from when the big thug had hit me with a hulking left hook. Looking down at my left side, I saw where the two bullets had hit me and were still lodged in the Kevlar and sticking into my skin. Sure, wearing the bulletproof vest had saved my life, but it still hurt like hell, feeling like I'd severely bruised that entire part of my body.

Reaching for my bloody dive knife resting two steps up from me, I wiped off the blood and slid it back into my sheath. Grabbing my Sig from my leg holster, I held it in both hands as I moved down the stairs, ready just in case more thugs had decided to join the party.

As I rounded the corner, I saw thug number four's enormous body lodged against the wall with his head tilted in an unnatural angle and his limbs sprawled out around him. Blood poured out from his open mouth as his body lay motionless.

"The bigger they are, the harder they fall," I said as I stepped over him. He'd been inches away from killing me, and I found myself thankful for all the hours I'd spent over the years doing leg presses in the gym.

# TWENTY

Reaching the bottom of the stairs, I climbed over the wreckage of shattered wood that was piled up in the doorway and stepped outside. With my Sig raised shoulder height, I did a quick scan of the area around me, looking for any sign of movement. There were two dead men just outside the doorway into the lighthouse, their bodies covered with blood and shrapnel as they lay motionless in the sand. The entire house had been consumed by a blazing inferno, with powerful yellow flames that burned so hot I could feel them on my exposed skin from over two hundred feet away.

As I moved my aching body to the other side of the lighthouse, doing a quick survey of the island, I saw that one of the dead men had been carrying a green Alejandro sniper rifle. I grinned as I crouched down, rolled the corpse over and picked up the Cuban-made long-range rifle, which had its standard PSO-1 scope attached to it. I did a quick inspection of the weapon to make sure that it was loaded and ready to fire, then holstered my Sig and held the sniper rifle in my hands as I stood up.

Looking over the portions of the island that were within view, it appeared as though that had been all of the thugs. As I glanced towards the eastern beach, I saw that one of the boats had left, but the other was still sitting idly in the surf, rocking up and down slightly with each crashing wave. Though my body hurt like hell and blood was starting to seep out through my bulletproof vest, I knew what I had to do.

Lumbering my way south towards the other side of the island, I soon reached the place where I'd left Chris and his family to hide. I let out a sigh of relief at seeing that their hiding place hadn't been disturbed at all since I'd left it. Stepping onto the large wooden sheet, I stomped my right heel three times, letting them know it was me. Then, in a loud voice, I yelled out my name a few times, just in case.

Falling to my knees, I pushed a few piles of the white sand aside, then shoved my fingers under the wood and pulled up. When I'd lifted it a few feet off the ground, I got some help from Cynthia, who was pressing her hands up against it. The four of them looked worried, and I could see that they'd been sweating a lot, all of their shirts almost soaked with it. It was now approaching 0700 and was probably already seventy degrees outside. And I knew that it would be much hotter in a tight space like the one they were hiding in.

"The island's clear for now," I said, catching my breath.

"Logan!" Cynthia said, staring at the blood oozing out from my left side. She stepped out of the hole and placed her hands on my bulletproof vest.

"You got shot?" she said, her eyes glancing up to look at mine.

"Yeah, twice," I said, trying to blow it off and not think about it, hoping that might make it a little more bearable.

"What do you mean, for now?" Chris asked. "I thought that was the last of them. I thought help was coming."

I shrugged. "There's no way of knowing." Then Cynthia started to remove the Velcro strap of my bulletproof vest, causing me to wince and step back. "It's fine!" I said sternly.

"No, it's not!" she fired back and closed the distance I'd put between us. "I need to stop the bleeding." She lifted up a portion of the vest. Then, telling me to hold still, she pulled out the bullets which were sticking about three-quarters of the way into my side. Grabbing a handkerchief from her back pocket, she dabbed some of the blood from my skin.

"There's no time," I said, waving her hands away from me and pulling the vest back over me. Grabbing the vest, she tucked the handkerchief under it, covering the wounds, and the tightness of the Velcro as I strapped it back down provided sufficient pressure to keep most of the blood at bay. It wasn't ideal, of course, but it would do for the time being. Then addressing all four of them, I said, "Stay on the island and be careful." I looked up over the northern tip of the island, focusing on the top portion of the ship which was all that was visible far off in the distance. Taking a few deep breaths, I added, "I'm going to the ship, and I'm gonna finish this."

I ushered Cynthia back into the hole and started to lower the wooden plank, but she stopped me. Holding her hands up against the mahogany, she stared deep into my eyes.

"Logan, stop!" she said. "Just wait. Calm down and think this over."

"I'm sick of waiting. You saw what those assholes did." I motioned to the thin line of smoke still rising up into the eastern sky, coming from the wrecked Coast Guard helicopter. "And they'll do it again when more help comes. No, I'm taking these guys down."

"But you're hurt. How can you even expect to make it onto that ship, let alone fight all of them?"

I took in a deep breath, then sighed. "I have to try."

Looking at the two young girls clutching their father's leg, I saw tears welling up in their eyes.

"Be careful, Logan," Alex said, sniffling and burying her face in her dad's chest.

Though it hurt like hell, I bent down beside her and said, "I will. I'm gonna get you and your family off this island. Even if it kills me, I'm gonna get you all out of here."

Rising back to my feet, I stared into Cynthia's teary eyes and nodded before turning and heading north, towards the other side of the island. As I passed by what remained of the burning house, I started to move in a crouch, keeping my body hidden from view behind the shrub line. Those assholes had made two very big mistakes. First, they'd blown that helicopter full of innocent Coast Guardsmen out of the sky, killing the three guys inside, including Ryan, a young married guy who'd recently had a baby. The second big mistake they'd made was that they'd sent a guy to the island carrying a sniper rifle. Bad idea.

When I reached a thick patch of bushes just a few hundred feet from the northern beach, I dropped down onto my stomach with the sniper rifle held in front of me. There was a soft breeze blowing through the grass and shrubs, allowing me to move without drawing attention to myself. I crawled towards a small sandbank, keeping my body as close to the ground as I could and trying to calm my breathing. When I'd crawled to the top of the sandbank, which was covered with thick green vines, I poked my head up over the sand and grass just enough to spot the ship still anchored about half a mile from shore, idly swaying in the current.

Sliding the sniper rifle slowly up over the sand, I rested it with the barrel sticking between the branches of a large shrub. Shutting my left eye, I pressed my cheek against the front end of the stock and focused through the PSO-1 scope with my right eye. Using my left hand, I adjusted the knobs on the top of the scope, zooming in on the ship and then bringing it into focus. The key to being a good sniper is to move slowly and methodically and to always control your breathing in a rhythmic, steady manner. It's surprising how difficult it can be to keep a target locked in your crosshairs from half a mile away when your heart is racing. In fact, it's damn near impossible.

My body was perfectly relaxed as I did a quick scan of the ship, keeping an eye out for the sniper who'd tried to take me down the previous night. The deck was surprisingly empty. There were two guys standing at the stern, talking to each other as they lit up their cigarettes, holding pistols in their hands as they paced back and forth. I could see the shadow of a guy through the glass window of the control tower, and as I drew my field of vision back down towards the deck, I saw two guys lying on their stomachs, one of them holding a sniper rifle resting on a bipod and the other staring through a pair of binoculars. They were sprawled out with their upper bodies just fitting through a hole in the port railing. Magnifying the scope a little more, I saw that the sniper had his barrel aimed straight in the direction of the island.

Similar to my .338 Lapua, the Alejandro is a bolt-action rifle, so I lifted the bolt handle upwards, then pulled the bolt back as far as it would go. Seeing that there wasn't a round already chambered, I pushed it all the way forward, then closed it, stripping a bullet from the eight-round magazine. Taking a deep, slow breath, I let it all out as my finger made contact with the metal trigger. With the sniper staring into his scope caught between the crosshairs, I squeezed the trigger. The large-caliber round exploded from the chamber with a loud, violent boom, soaring through the end of the barrel. Feeling the stock of the rifle jolt my shoulder back, I watched as the bullet flew the air.

Just under a second later, the round reached its destination, exploding into the sniper's head and spraying blood in all directions as his body jerked backward from the sheer force of it. Before the spotter had processed what had happened, I'd chambered another round, shifted my aim and fired a second bullet straight at him. Upon seeing his friend's head blow to pieces, he shifted his position, trying to crawl backward out of the small hole in the railing. But before he could come to his feet, the second bullet caught him straight in the chest, launching his body backward. When a 7.62mm-diameter bullet hits human flesh at over two thousand feet per second, it usually leaves an exit wound somewhere around the size of a bowling ball, so I knew the thug was down for the count.

Keeping my movements slow, I zoomed out and did a quick scan of the deck, looking for another target. The two guys who'd been standing aimlessly on deck had both dropped down and were taking cover behind the engine for the crane and a pile of metal drums. Drawing my aim back up to the bridge, I locked in on the figure of a man standing on the other side of the large, partially tinted window. He looked like he was holding a radio and barking out orders from what was probably their controlling station. Squeezing the trigger, I sent a third bullet hurtling through the air. It exploded through the window, shattering the glass to pieces as it burst through the thug's neck, knocking his body from view.

I drew my aim back to the deck and fired off a few more rounds at the two thugs crouching at the aft end of the ship, trying to spook them out of their hiding places. When they didn't budge, I took one more look around the ship, then jumped to my feet and ran towards the skiff the thugs had left during their last assault. The black rigid-hull inflatable boat rested idly, with most of its hull sitting on the white sandy beach while the aft end shifted up and down with the surf.

As I ran up to the boat, I realized that it was an MR-800 military-grade skiff with a Yamaha 350-horsepower engine attached to the stern that would rocket her through the water at over fifty knots. I set my sniper rifle on the bow next to an AK-47 the thugs had left, then grabbed hold of the rubber straps at the front of the inflatable pontoons and shoved the boat back into the small crashing waves. I climbed aboard when the stern was deep enough for the prop. Moving my aching body over to the console, I prepared to hotwire the thing, then realized that the geniuses had left the key stuck in the ignition.

Turning the key, I roared the Yamaha to life, then pulled back on the throttles, backing the skiff into the ocean. Once deep enough, I punched the throttles forward, accelerating the inflatable with ease as I maneuvered to put the ship straight in front of me.

# TWENTY-ONE

Holding speed at just over thirty knots, I gripped the helm tight with my left hand and grabbed my sniper from the deck with my right. I rested the barrel of the high-powered rifle on the metal frame of the windscreen and took intermittent glances through the scope, making sure none of the thugs thought it was safe to walk freely about the deck again. The water was calm as glass following the storm, minimizing the bouncing as I cruised through the water and making it easier to keep the gun steady.

Every now and then, my vision would blur and my mind would get hazy. I was well beyond tired. My body hurt and was sore all over, but I ignored it and stayed focused, knowing that I had a chance to take all of them out and put an end to their attacks for good. Scanning the decks, control tower and various other visible sections of the ship, I saw no sign of movement of any kind. There was nobody in sight.

After a little over a minute, I reached the ship and

cruised around the bow and then around to its port side. I set my sniper on the metal deck and reached for my Sig strapped to my leg holster, holding it up in front of me and aching for a chance to use it. After taking a quick lap around the old rusted ship, I pulled up against the port side, the pontoon making contact with the rusty hull. Idling the engine, I let go of the helm and took two steps before jumping towards the side of the ship, reaching up, and grabbing hold of the handrail with my left hand. Peeking over the side, I pointed my Sig, ready to fire at a moment's notice, as I scanned every inch of the deck.

There was no movement to be seen as I drew my gaze from the aft section, where the crane rose high into the air, to the forward section, where metal stairs led up to the various levels of the tower. I couldn't see anyone through the glass windows of the control room, and above the bow, the Bell 206 helicopter still sat idly on the helipad.

Gripping the handrail tightly, I pulled myself up and over, my soles landing softly on the metal deck. Holding my Sig out in front of me with both hands, I moved forward towards the tower. The ship was eerily quiet as I searched the deck, my eyes darting back and forth as I approached the metal stairs. The steps were faded, with sharp grooves for traction, and they squeaked as I took them two at a time, moving quietly to minimize the noise. I looked through the window of a second-level room before entering. Grabbing the metal handle, I pushed it up, then pulled open the heavy watertight door. With my Sig raised, I moved down a narrow hallway, peeking into rooms that looked like disorganized messes of desks, tables, chairs, and cabinets.

When I reached the other side of the hallway,

after verifying that each room was empty, I unlatched a door leading back outside and pushed it away from me. I decided to head up to the third level and check out the cockpit. If there weren't any thugs there either, that would mean that they were hiding out down in the crew's quarters, the cargo hold or the engine room. The last thing I wanted was to have to go searching the bowels of a big ship like this one, knowing there could be bad guys around any corner. No, I decided that if I didn't find anyone in the cockpit, I'd rethink my strategy and come up with a different plan of action.

With the heavy door pushed aside, I felt the warm tropical morning air brush against my face and heard the easy splashing of the ocean against the hull. As I stepped through the doorway, I was welcomed aboard by a Louisville Slugger swinging ferociously straight towards me from just around the corner. It happened so fast that I didn't have time to avoid it or to try and block it in any way. The metal barrel smashed into the upper part of my chest, sending my body flying backward and knocking the wind out of me. As I hit the metal floor behind me with a loud thud, I trained my right hand, which was still clasped around my Sig, towards the door. Just as I squeezed the trigger, the thug, a tall Latino guy wearing a black dress shirt and sunglasses, hit me again, this time slamming the barrel into my right hand just as a bullet exploded out, piercing his left shoulder.

My Sig flew from my grasp and rattled against the deck as sharp pain radiated from my right hand. The well-dressed thug with the baseball bat jerked sideways and grunted loudly in pain as he reached for the bullet wound to his left shoulder. Dark blood oozed out through his shirt as he gripped the bat with one hand and slammed it down towards my head. At the last second, I jerked my head sideways, avoiding the blow by just a few inches as the metal barrel whooshed past my ear and slammed to the floor with a loud ting. Grabbing the barrel, I held it against the floor as I kicked my right heel into the guy's forehead, shattering his sunglasses.

He looked dazed as I clamped my legs together on either side of his shins, forcing my right leg forward and my left back, leveraging his body towards the ground. The Louisville Slugger rattled from his hands as he slammed into the metal floor. Reaching as far as I could, I grabbed the rubber-coated handle and jumped to my feet. My opponent proved to be just as agile, whipping his body forward and his legs under him and landing on his feet in an athletic stance. Grabbing the metal frame of his shattered sunglasses, he growled at me and then threw them to the ground.

He was slightly taller than my six foot two inches and stood just in front of the doorway with his fists raised in front of his chest. Blood continued to drip out from the bullet wound to his left shoulder as he gritted his teeth. He snarled at me as I threw the bat at him, catching him off guard and causing his eyes to grow wide as it spun towards him. As he tried to block it, I lunged towards him, jumped like I was about to slam it home on a breakaway, then grabbed hold of the pipes overhead and swung my body. Caught off guard, he was helpless as both of my heels slammed forcefully into his chest, launching his large frame off the ground and hurtling him through the open doorway behind him.

The guy got some serious air before slamming onto the deck and tumbling into the starboard railing.

As I grabbed the bat and moved swiftly through the doorway to finish him off, he struggled to his feet, grunting and looking slightly disoriented as he looked up at me. Suddenly, he yelled out violently and sprinted straight for me like an Olympian upon hearing the starting gun. Throwing the baseball bat aside, I jumped out of his path of destruction, grabbed hold of his shirt collar and used a combination of his momentum and my own strength to slam his head into the glass covering a red emergency ax just beside the doorway, shattering it to pieces. Blood covered his face as shards of glass crashed to the deck at our feet. Wrapping my right hand around his neck, I forced him back and threw him chest first onto the deck. Turning around, I grabbed the ax with both hands, brought it high over my head, and slammed it hard into the thug's back.

He thrashed in pain as I pressed my foot against his back and pulled out the bloody blade. As his body shook and he struggled for air, I moved back into the hallway, bent over and grabbed my Sig from the floor. Heading back through the door, I quickly put the big guy out of his misery, sending a 9mm round right through his skull, causing a thick stream of blood to flow out and pool around his body as he went still as stone. I gasped for air, trying to shake off the powerful blows he'd landed to my chest and hand. Observing the fingers of my right hand, I tried to straighten them and then shut them, but even the slightest movement hurt like hell.

Regaining my focus, I looked around the outside of the ship, but even with all the commotion, there was no one else lumbering about. I took one more look at the bloodied thug before heading for the metal stairs to check the cockpit. Clearly, he wasn't one of

Salazar's goons who usually got his hands dirty, though he'd been trained extensively and was likely a top-tier assassin. No, most of Salazar's grunt workers were lying dead in the sand over on Loggerhead.

I made quick work of the stairs, reaching the top in seconds and scanning through the windows of the cockpit with my Sig raised to shoulder height. From my angle, I hadn't seen anyone inside or any movement at all. I moved for the watertight door, pushed up the metal locking device and pulled it open. It squeaked loudly, sounding even louder in the empty, quiet cockpit. Moving inside, I scanned behind a row of control panels, then circled a table in the center that was covered with charts and maps. The room had good natural lighting, with windows that circled all the way around and let in a blinding ray of morning sunshine as the sun rose up into the sky. As I passed by the helm, I saw the dead guy I'd shot with my sniper rifle lying on the floor in a pool of blood. Though he had lighter skin than the thug I'd chopped downstairs, he too wore a nice button-up shirt. Glancing up, I saw the bullet hole my rifle had made in the center of the glass.

Seeing that the room was clear, I knew that there was no place the others could be other than below decks. The idea of going down there and looking for them on their own turf and in dimly lit nooks and crannies didn't exactly excite me. As I walked around the counter and looked through the massive sheets of glass towards the aft section of the ship, I saw groups of large metal barrels strapped together along the port and starboard sides. I'd passed by them on my way up from the skiff but had just noticed for the first time how many there really were. Maybe I didn't have to go down below decks after all. Maybe I could get them to come out of their own accord.

Turning to my left, I headed for the watertight door I'd entered through, which was still wide open and letting in a soft tropical breeze that felt good against my face. When I was just a few steps from the doorway, I heard movement coming from the other side of the room, behind a set of control panels. Suddenly, two small but heavy objects rattled along the floor, heading straight for me. I recognized them instantly as grenades and instinctively dove to my right, taking cover behind a metal counter. Just as my body slammed into the hard floor, I heard a loud hissing sound, which was followed right after by a cloud of white gas shooting from the grenades and filling the air. Teargas, I thought as I quickly covered my mouth with the collar of my shirt. I jumped to my feet, but before I could reach the door, the small control room turned white, filling completely with the gas.

My eyes stung like hell and welled up with tears as I struggled to breathe, gagging short gulps of toxic air. I couldn't see anything as I backstepped towards the door, hoping to escape the white cloud of gas that was wreaking havoc on my face and lungs. Disoriented, I turned around and reached ahead of me. My hand grazed against the squeaky metal door just as a pair of arms wrapped around me from behind. I fired off two shots blindly into the gas with my Sig before my unknown enemy knocked the weapon from my hands. His powerful hands gripped my vest tight and slammed me down onto the floor with a loud thump. I caught only a glimpse of a black gas mask through the tear gas before I felt a jarring pain rattle across my skull as my unknown assailant slammed the butt of a rifle into my forehead.

# TWENTY-TWO

My mind was in a painful haze as strong arms turned me over and slammed me onto my chest. I could barely breathe as my hands were forced behind my back and my wrists locked together by what felt like a large plastic zip tie. I coughed and gagged as the thug grabbed me by the shoulders and dragged me through the doorway, out of the thick cloud of gas. The blinding rays of sunshine were painful as they beat against my watery eyes. I got only intermittent glimpses as a few more guys grabbed hold of me, helping to drag me along the grated walkway and down the creaking metal stairs.

Once back on the main deck, the thugs shoved me against the starboard bulkhead, then slapped me around a bit, trying to shake me out of it. I blinked my eyes a few times, then slowly opened them. They still hurt like hell from the teargas, but they were getting a little better each second. My breathing relaxed as my lungs enjoyed the sweet taste of fresh air. As my vision cleared, I saw that there were three guys standing in front of me. Two of them looked like they could be professional wrestlers, both having muscles that bulged out from their button-up dress shirts. The third was smaller, with a gold front tooth and—I don't know how else to say it—he looked like a guy you'd see in an insane asylum, the way his crazy eyes looked at me.

The two big thugs held handguns, one of them a Glock 19 and the other a Desert Eagle, and the crazy-looking dude with the gold tooth held a shotgun. By the way they watched me like a hawk, it was clear that they weren't messing around. And for good reason—they'd seen firsthand the damage I'd done to their buddies over the past day or so. I knew I wouldn't get an inch of slack from these knuckle draggers.

After leaning against the bulkhead for a few moments, a metal door opened loudly on the bottom level of the tower and a guy stepped out. As he walked nonchalantly towards us, he took intermittent drags of his massive cigar, which was burned about halfway. I instantly recognized him from the few images I'd seen on the news, the most prominent being a mugshot taken the day he had been captured in Miami. He reminded me of Al Pacino in *Scarface*, only older and with thick black chest hair that was visible underneath his half-unbuttoned red shirt. He had long dark hair and wore sunglasses that concealed his eyes completely. Around his neck, he wore two thick gold chains that clanked together as he moved. He wasn't very tall, maybe five seven, but he had a commanding presence that went beyond his size.

Strolling up alongside his goons, he eyed me from head to toe as he took a deep inhalation of his cigar and then blew it out into my face. The smoke stung my eyes a little, but I didn't give him the satisfaction of letting it show.

"So, this is the shithead who's been giving us so much trouble," he said, glancing at the three men standing beside him. He spoke with a strong Cuban accent, and he sounded pissed off. "Look at him," he continued, pointing a finger at me as he moved his head to look from one thug to the other. "This is the guy you call a demon. He's just a fucking man." Taking a step towards me, he hit me with a hard right, his two gold rings slamming into my jaw. As I grunted and gritted my teeth he added, "Just flesh and bones." He took a long drag of his cigar, then exhaled the smoke and continued, "Who sent you to protect them? FBI? CIA?"

"No one," I said, then spat out a gob of gooey mess that had built up in my mouth from breathing in the tear gas.

"No one?" he said, moving closer to me. Then, grabbing me forcefully by my shirt collar, he shook me violently. "You expect me to fucking believe that?"

I stared through the dark lenses of his sunglasses and replied, "It's true. I was trying to escape the storm when I heard gunshots."

"Oh, you just heard gunshots?" he said sarcastically, shaking his head. He gave a sinister laugh and added, "You've killed forty-four of my men since yesterday morning. Hale is useless. I saw the beating he got on camera yesterday. That means that you did it all alone. Like fucking hell nobody sent you."

"I wasn't alone," I said. "Chris's wife killed a few of your thugs." It was a slight exaggeration, but though she wasn't exactly Beatrix Kiddo, she had saved my life earlier that morning when she'd shot that thug in the head with her Beretta. "And," I continued, "I had a constant supply of firearms and other weapons. I guess I have you to thank for that, Salazar."

He wiped the smug smile from my face with another hard punch, this time to my right cheek. Pain screamed from my face, and I could almost feel the rage radiating from the gang leader's body.

"Well, you have failed them," he growled. "You were destined to fail the moment you fucked with me. I always get my way. You've got balls, I'll give you that. And you must be highly trained to have protected them all by yourself for so long. But I will have my way. Not even a maximum-security prison could keep me contained. You have fought hard, but in the end, you see, I always get my way. I will kill Christian, just like I killed that fat-ass judge. And as I swore to him as I was being dragged in chains to rot away for life in that cage, I will kill his wife and daughters as well."

The sound of radio chatter broke the silence that followed Salazar's evil and resolute declaration. One of the big thugs hovering over the side of me reached for a black radio that was clipped to the fancy leather belt looped into his dress pants.

Grabbing it, he listened a moment to words that I couldn't hear, then turned to Salazar and said, "There are transmissions." His eyes were wide as he listened for a few seconds more, then added, "They're sending two Coast Guard patrols this way. The American Navy base in Key West is also taking action." He held the radio out to Salazar, his hand shaking. "How are we gonna get out of this, boss?"

I wasn't surprised. I estimated that it had been at least forty minutes since the Coast Guard helicopter had gone down. Even if the pilots hadn't been able to get a distress signal out as it crashed to a fiery grave, it wouldn't have taken long for air traffic controllers at both the Coast Guard station in Key West and the Naval station to realize that something was wrong. I reasoned that Coast Guard patrols from Key West, a little over sixty miles away, could probably reach Loggerhead in just over an hour, meaning that they would be here soon.

Snatching the radio from the big guy's hand, Salazar threw it over the side. The sound of voices coming through the small speaker grew fainter, then went silent as the radio flew out of view, splashing into the water below.

"I don't give a damn who's coming," Salazar snarled. "We'll be back in Cuba in less than half an hour. And once we're there, we're home free. I already have a secure landing zone with full air support ready for us, along with a private jet ready to take us anywhere in the world."

Salazar strode nonchalantly towards the railing beside me. Then, taking one final drag from his cigar, he threw it over the side. Placing a hand on my shoulder, he lifted his sunglasses and stared at me with his dark brown eyes. "He who has the money has the power," he said.

Then he shot me an evil smile and moved over to one of the barrels of fuel latched to the railing. Grabbing it with two strong arms, he dragged it towards the center of the ship, then ripped off the plug. Pushing the top of the barrel, he knocked it over, sending fuel splashing to the deck and pooling near the center of the ship as it emptied. Glancing up at his three men, Salazar yelled at them, ordering them to empty the rest of the barrels as well. The three thugs jumped into action, grabbing the other barrels one by one and drenching the entire deck with the highly flammable liquid. The potent stench of the fuel hurt my nostrils, replacing the fresh sea air of the Caribbean.

As Salazar moved back towards my position against the starboard railing, he looked at the crazy-looking thug with the shotgun and said, "Start up the chopper, Steven." The guy nodded, then turned on his heels and ran towards the metal stairs.

Standing in front of me, Salazar looked at the big thug to his right and held out his hand. "Give me his weapons."

Without hesitation, the thug produced my Sig and dive knife from the back of his pants and handed them to Salazar. Salazar immediately took a step closer to me and then pulled back the hammer on my Sig, making it easier to pull the trigger. A moment later, he pointed the barrel at my head.

*This is it*, I thought as he gave me a crooked, evil smile. I had to do something, but with my wrists bound behind my back and my ankles lashed together, I knew that there was nothing I could do. I could barely move my body, let alone try and take him out before he pulled the trigger.

Tilting his head, he lowered my Sig, then stashed it in the back of his pants. "No," he said, "I'm not going to kill you."

Grabbing my dive knife, he held it up in front of me, its sharpened steel edge glistening in the bright tropical sun. In an instant, he wrapped a hand around my back and pulled me towards him. With my momentum forcing me closer to him, he stabbed the tip of my knife deep into my abdomen, the blade slicing far into the lower part of my rib cage. I gasped and grunted in pain as the blade pierced through me.

Grabbing me forcefully, Salazar brought his mouth close to my left ear and said, "No. Why get my hands dirty when I can let Mother Nature take care of you?"

As the words came out of his mouth, he ripped out my blade and stepped away from the railing. The two big thugs closed in on me, grabbing me on both sides and lifting me up to the top of the rail. I caught a glimpse of Salazar as he dug a Zippo out of the front pocket of his dress pants and flicked a flame alive. My body reaching the top of the railing, the two thugs hurled me over the side. I flew backward, twisting and spinning wildly as the bright sky and ocean blurred in and out of view. In the heat of the moment, a fraction of a second before breaking the surface, I forced a gulp of air deep into my lungs.

# TWENTY-THREE

I splashed into the warm Caribbean water headfirst, my body spinning and sinking about five feet under before the drag of the water slowed me to a stop. Keeping myself as calm as possible, I opened my eyes, squinting and feeling the slight sting as they adjusted themselves. Blood flowed out from my chest, and glancing down, I saw a deep gash where Salazar had stabbed me on the right side of my abdomen. I fought back the pain and took a second to think of a plan. Looking up, I saw the surface just a few kicks above me but knew that it would be a waste of time to surface. Even if I somehow managed to get back onto the ship, Salazar or one of his thugs would riddle me with bullets just as I reached the deck. Feeling the thick plastic of the zip ties cutting off the circulation in my ankles and wrists, I knew I had to find a way to break free before doing anything else.

I drew my gaze down towards the seafloor and spotted patches of elkhorn and brain coral about ten feet below me. Shifting my upper body down and my legs back, I kicked as best as I could, slithering my body through the water. The pain in my side was almost unbearable as I forced my body to propel itself down. A thick stream of dark red trailed behind me, branching out and dissipating into the ocean. A shark can detect even the smallest amounts of blood in the water, and if there happened to be one close by that decided to attack me while my arms and legs were restrained, I'd have no way to fight it off.

Upon reaching the bottom, I equalized my ears to the pressure, then found a large growth of pillar coral rising up from the reef about twenty feet away from me. Pillar coral is a hard coral that resembles fat fingers growing up from the seafloor. This particular coral was beige and rose up about seven feet from the sand below. Having cut myself a few times in my life swimming a little too close to hard coral, I knew firsthand just how sharp it could be. Swimming up close to one of the outlying pillars, I extended my hands as far back behind me as they could go, then pulled my hands away from one another and pressed the plastic zip tie against its sharp ridges. Bending my elbows, I seesawed the plastic up and down, scraping it forcefully against the razor-sharp coral. The commotion spooked what looked like a decent-sized pompano fish out of its hiding place, causing it to skirt past me, its silver body sparkling in the sun. After a few seconds, I felt the plastic start to crack, and then it snapped in an instant, sending my hands flying out to my sides.

With my hands free, I grabbed hold of the coral carefully and went to work on the zip tie holding my ankles together. As the plastic snapped, freeing my legs, I looked up towards the surface for the first time in about a minute and a half. Near the hull of the ship, there was a dark red cloud spreading out in all directions. With my vision blurred I couldn't tell what it was, but Salazar's thugs had thrown a bloodied piece of animal flesh into the ocean, just in case my bleeding chest wasn't enough to attract every shark for miles.

Knowing I had to do something to try and slow the amount of blood I was losing, I slipped my tee shirt over my head and tied it around my abdomen. It wasn't ideal by any means, but it slowed the bleeding. Taking a moment to look around the seafloor and at the anchored ship above, I quickly got my bearings and used what remained of the air in my lungs to swim towards Loggerhead. I'd already been down for at least three minutes, but I wanted to put as much distance between myself and the ship as possible.

After I'd kicked my way over the reef about a hundred feet from the ship, I glanced up and saw the black inflatable boat drifting lifelessly, the current taking it south. As I swam up closer, I realized that it had been deflated, no doubt by Salazar's men. But even destroyed, it could still help me. As fast as I could, I rose up out of the water, crawled over the loose flaps of rubber, and grabbed the AK-47, then took a deep breath and vanished back beneath the surface.

Kicking my feet and stroking with my left arm, I swam back down to the bottom and kept moving towards the shore. It felt good to at least have a weapon in my hands, but that feeling was short-lived as I spotted a shark swimming my direction from the southwest. I couldn't tell what kind it was since my vision was so blurred from not wearing a dive mask, but judging by the way it moved towards me, it was looking to feed.

With my body a painful wreck and my side hurting so bad I could barely move, I forced myself to keep kicking and stroking my arms, propelling myself as fast as I could through the water towards the shore. My lungs throbbing for air, I forced myself up towards the surface, having spent what felt like an eternity beneath the waves. Barely breaking the surface, I sucked in a quick lungful of air and took a brief look around before dropping right back down. Behind me, the entire deck of the ship was going up in flames, sending thick black clouds of smoke into the air. Overhead, I heard the distinct sound of Salazar's helicopter as it roared towards the center of Loggerhead. I knew full well what he was going to do when he found Chris and his family. Unable to get their faces out of my mind, I forced myself to move faster, pulling my arms through the water with strong, methodical strokes and scissor-kicking my legs back and forth.

I kept myself about five feet from the surface, and when I was halfway between the ship and the sandy white beach of Loggerhead, I spotted another shark circling around me. The trail of blood continued to flow out of my side even with my shirt tightened against it, making me wonder how much I'd lost. It made me dizzy just thinking about it, so I pushed it out of my mind and kept moving, keeping a watchful eye on the two sharks, making sure neither of them had decided to come at me.

A few seconds later, one of the sharks swam straight for me and then veered off once he'd reached about ten feet away. Seeing it closer, I could tell it was a tiger shark, an aggressive shark that can grow up to fifteen feet long and is second only to great whites in its number of recorded attacks on humans. Glancing ahead, I knew that I still had a quarter of a mile to swim before I'd reach land. There was no way a grown tiger shark would let a bleeding creature swim that far without making a move.

Keeping my head on a swivel, I watched the two sharks attentively, preparing myself for their next pass at me. What pissed me off the most was that I liked sharks. I'd been diving with tiger, great white and bull sharks hundreds of times before and had never been attacked. In truth, I'd always thought that sharks were fascinating and greatly misunderstood creatures. But I knew that with blood in the water, it was a different story. Even a friendly shark could become like a rabid dog and come after you in the blink of an eye upon getting a whiff of fresh blood.

Casting my blurry gaze on the largest of the two sharks, I slowed to a stop, watching eagerly as it flapped its tail fin, swimming straight for me. The most important thing is to remain calm, so I forced myself to be as relaxed as possible as the shark moved in. When it was within a few feet of me, its jaws sprang open, revealing rows of sharp white teeth. Not wanting to severely hurt the animal, I slugged it in the nose with the butt of my AK-47 just as it was about to find out what my thigh tasted like. The massive predator freaked out and darted away from me as fast as it could. The other circling tiger shark, seeing his buddy get his nose punched in, kept his distance and only swam towards me a couple of times as I turned and kicked for the shore. But he never swam in close enough to strike.

By the time I reached the shore, my body was an aching and exhausted wreck. I'd lost so much blood that my mind was delirious and my body tried desperately to go into shock. But I sure as hell wasn't gonna stop. I'd pushed myself beyond my limits, but I had to push a little bit more if I was going to save Chris and his family. It's in the moments of sheer pain and exhaustion, when your body screams at you that it can't go on anymore, that you find out what you're really made of. You realize that you're capable of more than you'd ever believed. You realize that there's another level when you push, breaking through the self-generated barriers and limitations of your existence. Gritting my teeth and heaving my body through the surf, I forced my way through those barriers, punching through them like I was going for a knockout in the twelfth round.

As I stepped out of the ocean, lumbering through the fine white sand, I heard the sounds of the helicopter, its rotor rattling through the air. Hoping that I wasn't already too late, I picked up the pace as much as my body would allow. As I moved past the shrub line, I saw the top of the helicopter as it idled on the clearing beside the lighthouse. All I could think about was their faces, all four of them, and how they needed me right then. I planned for the worst, expecting the helicopter to take off and fly high into the sky at any moment, leaving me to do nothing but watch as the family I'd struggled so hard to protect flew off to their certain deaths.

Large drops of water and blood dripped down from my shorts and tee shirt, splattering across the sand as I kept my body low, moving in towards the helicopter while keeping my head on a swivel and my eyes peeled for Salazar and his men. I gripped the black AK-47 firmly in my wet hands, aiming it forward as I trudged over a small sand dune covered in shrubs. I forced my legs to keep working, and soon

I was within a few hundred feet of the base of the lighthouse and the helicopter idling just behind it. To my surprise, the old white house was still burning, though the flames had dwindled to just a few small piles of dark rubble.

As I crouched behind the lighthouse for cover, I heard voices coming from the direction of the helicopter. Stepping my way around the round base, I spotted one of the big thugs and watched as he reached for the side door, grabbed the handle and slid it open forcefully. Moving another step around the base of the lighthouse I saw two more, along with Salazar, and they were forcing Chris and his family towards the helicopter as their hands were pressed against the back of their heads. Looking closer, I realized that their hands were zip-tied the same way mine had been before Salazar had stabbed me and thrown me overboard to die.

I inched around the corner, then knelt down and pressed the butt of the AK against my shoulder, aiming at the first thug. I didn't have a good shot. Since the helicopter was practically facing me, half of the big guy's body was covered by the front end of it. But as Salazar led Chris and his family closer, I knew I only had a few seconds to make a move, or else they'd be history. Not daring to risk the possibility of a stray bullet, I switched the AK-47's rate of fire to semiautomatic by pressing the metal switch on its side all the way down. Then, putting the big thug's head directly in my sights, I took in a deep breath and pulled the trigger.

The bullet rocketed through the air, exploding into the thug's face and launching his body backward. Immediately after pressing the trigger, I shifted my aim to the other massive thug and pressed the trigger again, shooting a bullet straight into his chest before he realized what was happening. Salazar yelled at the top of his lungs as he aimed his pistol in my direction, firing rounds straight at me.

I turned and performed a painful roll backward and to my right, narrowly avoiding his bullets as they slammed into the side of the lighthouse. Regaining my balance, I forced myself into a run, moving around to the other side of the lighthouse and hearing more bullets fired my way, including a few shotgun blasts from the crazy-looking skinny thug. When I reached the other side, I knelt down, took a breath and popped out. The skinny thug was already sitting in the cockpit, his hands going to work, pressing buttons and grabbing hold of the controls. Salazar was freaking out, yelling and cursing wildly over the whipping sounds of the main rotor as he forced the young family to board the helicopter at gunpoint.

From my angle, Salazar was behind the family, so I had no other choice but to get closer. With my AK raised and my sights panning back and forth between Salazar and Skinny, I made my move, rushing towards the helicopter. When I was about fifty feet from the chopper, Salazar spotted me, his eyes growing wide with the realization of who was trying to take them out. *That's right*, I thought. *It's me, the guy that you should have killed.*

I could see the panic in his eyes as he grabbed Cynthia, who was the nearest family member to him, wrapped his left arm around her neck and pressed a revolver against the side of her head. I tried to get the gang leader in my crosshairs, but he did a good job keeping his body hidden behind the others.

"Drop the fucking gun!" he yelled, staring into my eyes as he took a step backward towards the open side door of the helicopter. He grabbed Cynthia tighter, and though I could see the fear in her eyes, I also saw a hint of rage as he jerked her head side to side while he forced her back. "Drop it now or she's dead."

For a split second, I debated pulling the trigger. I was confident in my aim, but I also knew that he could jerk her body at the last second, placing her directly in my line of fire as I was squeezing the trigger. I knew that I wouldn't be able to live with myself if I killed her, even if it was an accident.

"You've got two seconds!" he barked over the loud spinning rotors as the backs of his legs hit the side of the helicopter.

I gritted my teeth and narrowed my gaze as I bent my knees slowly, lowered the AK and then dropped it onto the sand at my feet.

Seeing the rifle out of my hands, Salazar forced Cynthia to step up into the helicopter, climbing in right beside her. Once they were seated, with Cynthia on the end, blocking my view, he looked over at me and said, "You just don't fucking learn, do you, guy?"

My eyes grew wide and my heart raced as Salazar pulled his revolver off Cynthia's head and aimed it at Chris, who was standing just to my right, barely able to stay on his feet with his broken right leg.

"Keep her on the ground for another minute," Salazar yelled at Skinny, who had his head turned back, watching the ordeal take place behind him. He nodded, and with the barrel still aimed at Chris, Salazar continued, "You really screwed up." Shaking his head, he added, "Now you have to watch them die. One by one." He shot me an evil smile as he pulled back the hammer of his revolver. "And you," he said, staring at Chris. "You brought this upon yourself. Well, I hereby sentence you to death by firing squad."

Just as Salazar started to squeeze the trigger, Cynthia slammed her head into his hands and bit down, clamping her front teeth into the loose skin between his left thumb and index finger. The bullet exploded from Salazar's revolver, narrowly missing Chris as it whizzed past his face and made contact with the beach twenty feet behind him, spraying up a pile of loose sand. Salazar yelled in pain as blood flowed out of his hand. Before he could react to Cynthia's act of bravery, I was already lunging towards the helicopter, my body acting instinctively.

As I ran, forcing my body towards the helicopter, Cynthia struggled with Salazar, trying to slam the revolver out of his hands. Skinny upped the speed of the rotors drastically, and I reached the chopper just as its landing skids started to lift off the ground. Taking one final big stride, I forced my right foot into the sand, pushing as hard as I could and launching my body high into the air. I flew into the cabin, my body hurtling past Cynthia and into Salazar, knocking him hard into the glass window of the other side door. Grabbing his right hand, which was still gripping the revolver, I smacked it against the back of the seat in front of us, causing it to rattle onto the rubber mat under our feet and then tumble out of the open door beside us.

As Salazar reached for his fallen weapon, I smashed his head into the wall, causing his nose to crunch and blood to flow out. His bloodied left hand was still wrapped forcefully around Cynthia's neck, and as I reached to break her free, I saw Skinny out of the corner of my eye. His upper body was turned around and he was arcing his shotgun straight for me. He was some kind of stupid to use a weapon like that in a helicopter, but I knew that wouldn't stop the bullets from tearing a hole eight inches wide through the center of my chest. A fraction of a second before the barrel pointed at me, I grabbed hold of it and pried it free from his scrawny arms.

"Logan!" Cynthia yelled, and as I turned to look back at Salazar, I realized that he'd snatched my dive knife from the back of his pants and was stabbing it straight towards me. Reacting as fast as I could, I deflected the blow, redirecting it away from its intended target of my neck. But I wasn't able to deflect it completely in the compact space, and it stabbed painfully into my left leg, cutting in about two inches.

As I gritted my teeth in pain, I grabbed hold of his right hand and punched him twice square in the face. His head jerked back, and as he loosened his grip on Cynthia, I ripped the knife from his hands and snatched her from his grasp. With her shaking body held tightly in my arms, I stabbed Skinny through the side of his skull, causing blood to gush out and his body to shake violently. As I turned back to Salazar, his eyes were massive in his bloodied face. He yelled out barbarically and lunged at us. As I stabbed him in the chest with the knife, he pushed us both towards the left side of the cabin. Unable to stop our momentum, we tumbled out the open door and free-fell towards the beach below.

Holding Cynthia in my arms, I landed in a way that would ensure that my body would take most of the damage as we crashed into the sand with a loud thud. It hurt, but not as bad as I'd thought it would, and as I glanced up at the chopper, I realized we'd only fallen about ten feet. My body screamed in pain from the wound to my leg as I watched the helicopter flying wildly just overhead. With a stern gaze, I watched as Salazar struggled into the cockpit and pushed Skinny aside, taking over at the controls.

"You've got to be kidding me," I said as Salazar stabilized the chopper and started to gain altitude. Willing my body to move, I searched the beach around me for a weapon. Then, seeing Salazar's revolver resting in the sand just in front of me, I crawled on my hands and knees, dragging my aching body over to it. I grabbed hold of it and, lifting my head up, I took aim at the chopper, which was now at least a hundred feet overhead and climbing fast. Squeezing the trigger, I sent round after round into the tail section, aiming for the rear rotor assembly. I hoped to give him a taste of the same medicine his thugs had given the Coast Guard helicopter earlier that morning.

The bullets rattled and sparked on contact, and after the first four shots, the rotor started to send out small plumes of black smoke. The final round in the revolver hit the rear rotor dead on, causing it to break off the tail section and fall lifelessly to the beach below. Without the rear rotor, it would be almost impossible for the helicopter to fly as there would be no counter torque for the main rotor. The chopper spun wildly a few times before, miraculously, Salazar managed to bring it somewhat stable. It was a few hundred feet up and moving west, bobbing up and down and side to side but staying in the air as it cruised towards the open ocean.

With the white smoke from the final round of the revolver still rising up from the barrel, I dropped it back onto the sand. My eyelids felt impossibly heavy, and my body hurt so bad I felt like it could be the end for me. I'd lost a lot of blood, probably far too much to survive. After everything my body had been through, the racked-up hours without sleep, being shot and stabbed multiple times, and feeling as if every corner of my body had been bruised, it finally gave out. As Salazar piloted the damaged helicopter wildly into the western horizon, my eyes closed and my face fell into the sand.

# TWENTY-FOUR

I woke up to the sound of rhythmic beeping and, after slowly opening my eyes, I saw that there was a heart monitor machine just a few feet from my face. Blinking my eyes a few times, I cleared the blurriness out of my vision and moved my head gently from side to side. I was lying on my back in a hospital bed with a white blanket covering my body and rubber tubes sticking out of my arms.

Looking around, I saw that the room had two green padded chairs, a metal cabinet and a TV mounted on the wall across from me that looked like it hadn't been used in a while. To my right, there was a door propped open by a black rubber doorstop. I heard the faint sounds of chatter and a distant phone ringing, but it was quiet for the most part. To my left, there was a good-sized window with its beige plastic blinds shut, allowing me to see only a glimpse of bright sunlight and green bushes full of colorful flowers on the other side.

Hearing footsteps approach the door, I tilted my head back to the right and saw a petite nurse with short red hair walk by the open doorway, holding a clipboard in her hands and writing a quick note with her pen. She glanced towards me and, seeing that I was awake, turned on her heels and walked up to my bed.

"Welcome back," she said, shooting me a friendly smile as she set the clipboard on the counter beside my bed. She was pretty, and she looked to be in her mid-twenties. "Are you comfortable?" she added as she did a quick check of my vital signs. "Any pain whatsoever?"

Though my side still hurt pretty bad, even considering the meds they probably had me on, and my head was dizzy, I said only, "I'm fine. Thank you."

She smiled. "I saw your wounds, Mr. Dodge, and you're either the toughest man alive or you're lying to me right now."

I chuckled slightly, then stopped, realizing it was making the pain in my side worse. "I guess it hurts a little."

"Well, now, that's more like it," she said. "Just let us know if it's too intense so we can numb it down for you." She grabbed her clipboard, penned in a few remarks and added, "Well, everything looks good. You seem to be healing nicely. I'll let Dr. Patel know you're awake."

She gave me one more smile before turning and moving with light feet through the open doorway. Less than a minute later, a short Indian guy in his late fifties with gray hair walked in, wearing a white lab coat and glasses.

"Nice to see you're awake, Mr. Dodge," the man

said, smiling at me as he looked over my body from head to toe. Standing at the foot of my bed, he continued, “Thankfully, your vest stopped the bullets from doing any serious damage. But you suffered a pretty good blow to your head, a broken bone in your right hand, bruises all over your body and lacerations to both your side and your leg. The wound to your side was inches away from missing your kidney, and the one to your leg narrowly missed your femoral artery. All told, you’re lucky to be alive, Mr. Dodge.”

“Thanks,” I replied, my voice raspy and my mouth dry. “How long was I out for?”

He turned around, opened the metal cabinet and pulled out a bottle of water. Untwisting the cap, he stepped over and handed it to me. “The five of you came in here on Tuesday afternoon, and it’s now Thursday morning.”

Suddenly, a fog lifted from my mind and I sprang into action, thinking about Chris and his family. As I sat up, he placed a hand gently on my shoulder.

“They’re fine,” he said, reading my mind. “A little flustered and banged up, but nothing time won’t heal.”

My body relaxed a little and I dropped my head slowly back into my pillow.

“Are they here?”

He shook his head. “They checked out yesterday. The only one who was injured was the father, and he wanted to be treated by his doctor in Miami. They wanted me to tell you how grateful they are that you saved them. And they really meant it, Mr. Dodge.”

I smiled. “Call me Logan.”

“Well, Logan, there’s a few people out in the lobby waiting to see you. Do you want me to let them know you’re awake?”

"As long as it's not the police," I said, not knowing if I could handle both a hospital and law enforcement at the same time. He looked at me skeptically, so I smiled and said, "Only kidding."

He gave a faint smile, then patted me on the shoulder. "I'm glad you're alright, and just so you know, I'd like you to stay another day. Maybe two, depending on how your wounds look. You did a good thing saving that family, for what it's worth."

"Thanks, Doc."

"Call me Arjun," he said, and I nodded cordially as he turned and left the room.

*Another day or two?* I thought as I was left to myself. I shook my head and remembered why I couldn't stand hospitals. It wasn't that I wasn't grateful for them saving my life. I just didn't like being in a hospital any longer than I absolutely had to. Some people just aren't meant for it, I suppose. I think it's the smell more than anything else.

A minute later, Scott appeared at the door wearing nice pants, a light blue dress shirt, and a black tie. He looked well rested and relieved to see me alive and well. It was hard to believe that we had been hunting pythons together in the Everglades less than a week ago. He looked focused as he entered, then, seeing that I was alright, he let out a deep breath and smiled.

"You gave us quite the scare," he said, moving up to my bed. "If it had been anyone else, I might have been worried." I grinned as best as I could and he continued, "Shit, I wish I could've been there to have your back, brother. I flew down from D.C. as soon as they received your transmission." He placed a hand on my shoulder. "You did good, Logan. You did real good. Single-handedly taking out that many gang members is incredible, even for you. And Lord knows there's a young family that's alive and well, all thanks to you."

"Unfortunately," I said, sitting up on the bed and propping a pillow behind my back for support, "I took out one gang member too few."

His eyes darted to the floor and he nodded slightly. Just as he opened his mouth to say something, another guy walked up to the open door. *Here it comes*, I thought as I glanced over and saw Sheriff Wilkes walk through the doorway with confident strides, staring at me. He was wearing his full Key West Police uniform, and he had a serious look on his dark, aged face. I'd dealt with law enforcement enough times to know that I was in for hours of questioning and stacks of papers a foot high for all of my statements after everything that had happened on Loggerhead. I knew they'd just be doing their job, and I'd always respected the hell out of what they do, but man is it a hassle to deal with.

"Nice to see you're up," he said with a serious tone. "Quite the heroic act, saving that family. I've gotten all of their stories, and we're ready to hear your side of things as soon as you're able."

"Yeah, about that," I said. "Doc says I need to stay here a few more days and recover."

He nodded, "Yes, I spoke with him as well." Then, shaking his hand in the air, he added, "I guess there will be plenty of time for statements in the next couple of days. Just don't go anywhere until we've got everything figured out, alright?" Instead of waiting for me to answer, he continued, "Now, Salazar is still out there somewhere. Most likely he's shark food by now, but do you have any idea where he might've escaped to? We know that he couldn't have made it back to Cuba. Their military has had ships scouring the waters between here and Havana for the past two days."

After a short pause, I glanced at him and said, "The hell if I know." Then, shrugging, I added, "Probably dead. Like you said."

The sheriff eyed me with a narrowed gaze and then bit his lip. "Well, you get better now." He gave both me and Scott a final nod, then turned to leave. Before stepping through the open doorway, he turned his head and said, "I'll have one of my deputies in the waiting area, just in case you decide you're ready to make your statements." I didn't reply, and he disappeared out the door and down the hallway.

After a brief silence, Scott said, "Once you're up on your feet, I think a few dives and lunch at Salty Pete's are in order. You can tell me all about why the IRS shouldn't have your ass for destroying that house."

He laughed, and I smiled and said, "That house was begging to be burned down."

We both sat and talked a few more minutes before he said, "Well, that nurse keeps walking by and eyeing me. Looks like they want me to let you rest. I'll be in town a few more days. If there's anything you need, anything at all, just let me know." He placed his hand on my shoulder, then moved to the door.

"Well, there is one thing you could do," I said, my words freezing him in his tracks. Turning on his heels, he waited a moment, and then I continued, "You can get me the hell out of here."

Scott shook his head, giving me a confused smile. But seeing the seriousness in my eyes, he said, "Are you crazy? You almost got killed. You just said you—"

"I know where he is," I said, cutting him off.

He looked at me skeptically, then stepped through the door, shutting it behind him. "Salazar?" he said, raising his eyebrows at me. "Are you sure?"

"Yeah."

"Logan, what the hell? Why didn't you tell him, then?" When I didn't reply he sighed and said, "Sheriff Wilkes is a good man, you know that. He had a long career with the FBI. The man's a living legend."

"Yeah, well, he's also bound by his position."

"And I'm not?" he said, shaking his head. "I mean, shit, Logan. I'm a senator, for God's sake."

"That means you know as well as anyone exactly what will happen if I tell them where he is. He'll be captured, taken to trial and thrown right back into prison. Nine Cuban guards were killed during his first prison break. How many will it be the next time around? How many guys have been manipulated to fight and die for him? No, I won't tell a soul where he is, because he's mine. I'm going to hunt him down and I'm going to kill him, because it has to be done, Scott."

Scott stared at the floor, thinking over everything I'd said. "There's a lot of eyes on this one, Logan. I can't just go sneaking you out of the hospital to track down a gang leader who's probably already dead anyway. And you heard Wilkes, he's got a deputy here to keep tabs on you."

"He's not dead," I said. "I shot the tail, Scott. I saw the damage done, saw the rear rotor fall to the beach and the black smoke spitting out of the boom. His chopper had maybe three minutes of flight time max. No more. His chopper crashed, and he's still alive."

"And you're telling me you know where he is? How?"

"Look, I'm going to get out of here, and I'm going to go hunt him down whether you help me or not. But help me get out of here unseen and I'll tell you."

Scott eyed me with a frustrated gaze, then shook his head and took a few steps towards the doorway. He took a quick look through the small window, then walked back to my bed.

"Alright, have it your way," he said, then threw his hands in the air. "I'll help you out of here on one condition. If he wants to come quietly and surrender, we won't kill him. Understand?" I didn't exactly agree to it, but he continued anyway. "Now, what's the plan?"

Ten minutes later, I was out of bed and dressed in a pair of gray coveralls, complete with a ballcap that I kept low, covering most of my face. Fortunately, Ted the maintenance guy and I were about the same size, and he had a few extra uniforms stashed away in the nearby utility closet. I walked right out the back door of the hospital, meeting Scott, who sat in his black SUV, which he kept idled beside a dumpster and a wooden fence.

Opening the door, I hopped into the passenger seat and glanced at Scott, whose eyes were now shielded by a pair of dark Oakley sunglasses.

"This seems a little unnecessary," he said, grinning from ear to ear.

"Yeah, right. You heard the sheriff. That guy's watching me like a hawk. If he knew I was leaving, he'd have me tailed for sure. Then we'd never be able to go and get Salazar."

Looking over at me, as I slammed the door shut, he raised his hands and said, "Well, where to, Ted?"

I laughed. "To the marina."

He nodded, put the SUV in drive and drove out of the parking lot. On the way to the marina, we passed by a garage sale on White Street, and I spotted a kayak resting in the grass beside the curb.

"Hey, pull over, will you?" I said, pointing at the small paved driveway littered with plastic tables that were covered with various knickknacks.

Scott raised his eyebrows. "You really think now's the time for antiquing?"

Opening the door, I chuckled, turned back to Scott and said, "My wallet went to visit Davy Jones. You don't happen to have a hunk of cash on you, do you?"

A minute later, I was handing a round-bellied guy wearing one of those neon green visors a stack of four hundred-dollar bills. Then Scott and I folded down the back row of seats and loaded the two-person sit-atop kayak along with a pair of paddles into the back.

"What do we need that for?" Scott asked as we climbed back into the front seats of the SUV.

I looked through the windshield at the blue ocean, which was just visible between a break in the houses and palm trees. "You'll see."

# TWENTY-FIVE

It took us five minutes to get the Baia ready to go, unhooking the power cables and water lines before untying the mooring lines from the cleats on the dock and shoving off. I'd changed out of the maintenance uniform and into a pair of cargo shorts, a cutoff tee shirt, and my black Converse low-tops. We'd used ratchet straps to keep the kayak in place along the port side of the boat, where it would be easy to drop into the water when the time came. Starting up the twin six-hundred-horsepower engines, I brought her out of the Conch Marina and into the open ocean.

At just after 1100, it was already over eighty degrees, with just a small handful of patchy, white clouds far out above the horizon. As I brought her up on plane and accelerated her just past her cruising speed of thirty-five knots, I turned to Scott, who was seated on the white half-moon cushioned seat beside me.

"Here, grab the helm for a minute, will ya?" I

said as we were just passing Sunset Key. I stepped down into the salon and, opening one of the small cabinets above the stove, I pulled out a bottle of fast-acting extra-strength Advil. Popping the bottle open, I threw two pills down the hatch and chased them down with a few swigs of water, trying to numb the pain as whatever the hospital had given me started to wear off.

Stepping back outside, I slid open one of the large storage compartments on the port side and pulled out a long and narrow yellow object that looked like a torpedo. I spent a moment looking it over, making sure that it powered on without any hiccups and that the line connecting it to the boat was in good shape. I performed routine maintenance on all my equipment, so I was fairly certain that it would work just fine.

"Good idea," Scott said, glancing back at me as I placed the magnetometer on the deck just aft of the sunbed. "There's no way in hell that thing would miss a freaking helicopter." I nodded. It was top-of-the-line, which meant that it could detect a bottle cap a hundred feet down with ease.

I switched places with Scott, taking over at the helm, and stretched out her legs, rocketing her through the water at over fifty knots. The calm sea shot by us in a windy blur as we moved due southwest on a direct course for Dry Tortugas. In just over an hour, we passed Fort Jefferson and then cruised onward past Loggerhead Key. Staring at the long, skinny island, I couldn't help but think about the events that had transpired there. I had been close to biting it a few times, too close. Examining the island as best as I could, I saw a black pile of rubble in the center of the island, marking all that remained of the old white house. There was no salvage vessel in sight. Either it had sunk from the fire or, more likely, it had been towed up north to be scrapped.

I drew my gaze to the western horizon. When I'd fallen from Salazar's chopper, grabbed his revolver and fired off shots in his direction, he'd been heading west. And as the ammo had run out, I remembered watching the damaged helicopter continue in that direction until I'd passed out. Less than a mile from Loggerhead, I eased back on the throttles, bringing her to an easy thirty knots, and threw the magnetometer into the water. As we dragged the yellow device behind us, I had Scott open up my laptop and observe, looking for any signs of the lost helicopter.

Scott stared at the screen for a few minutes, then looked out over the water in front of us and said, "So where are we going, Dodge?"

I adjusted our course slightly. "As I told you at the hospital, Salazar's helicopter couldn't have made it more than a few minutes in the air after he left Loggerhead."

Scott shrugged, "So, what? He crashed somewhere and drifted aimlessly?"

"Or he found land."

Scott shook his head, "I wasn't aware that there was any land west of Dry Tortugas. Not for a hell of a long ways anyway."

"There is one island," I said, spotting the cliffs on the horizon in front of us just as I spoke the words. "And he would have seen it, and most likely he'd have aimed for it."

"What island?"

I glanced at Scott, then nodded in front of us. "That island."

Sliding out of the half-moon seat, he planted his feet on the deck, stood up and focused his gaze far out ahead of us. "What, that pile of rocks?"

"To a bloodied guy without a boat, that pile of rocks would probably look a hell of a lot better than a swim back to Dry Tortugas or to Havana," I said. "Besides, there's more to that island than meets the eye."

As I approached the island, I eased back on the throttles, bringing her down to about fifteen knots before hitting the reef line. A pod of bottlenose dolphins swam up along the starboard side, putting on a spectacular show as they glided through the water, occasionally jumping high into the air and landing with a smooth splash. As I admired the incredible creatures, marveling at how graceful and easy their movements were, the computer came to life, making more noise than the Tin Man walking through a security checkpoint.

I pulled back on the throttles, idling the Baia, then moved back onto the swim platform to have a look. Scott, who'd also been curious as to what the magnetometer was detecting, was standing right beside me, peering through the surface of the clear water. About forty feet down, there was a strange-looking dark object that we both instantly realized was the Bell 206 helicopter Salazar had taken off in. I patted Scott on the back, then opened a small storage compartment and pulled out a clear Cressi dive mask.

Slipping out of my tee shirt and shoes, I said, "Hold her steady for a moment." Then, strapping on the mask, I added, "I gotta see if he's still down there."

Though Doc had insisted I take it easy for a few more days, I could think of no better way to reinvigorate my body than a jump into warm tropical water. Hurling my body over the end of the swim platform, I splashed down headfirst and reached the helicopter in a few smooth strokes. It was on its left side, and its rotor was jammed against a large lobe coral. Thankfully, all of its windows were shattered, making it easy for me to navigate in through the windshield frames. A quick glance revealed that the helicopter was completely empty.

I looked around for a few more seconds, just to see if there were any clues, and when I didn't find any, I kicked my way back up to the surface. Breaking up into the warm fresh air, I slid my mask down to hang around my neck and grabbed the ladder attached to the swim platform.

"Well?" Scott said as he offered his hand to help me up.

I shook my head. "Looks like we're going hunting."

After toweling off, I decided to mark the location of the sunken helicopter on my GPS, just for future reference in the unlikely event I forgot where it was. When I was finished, I pushed the throttles forward, cruising around to the northwestern side of the island, then killed the engine and dropped anchor right at the edge of the reef, about a quarter of a mile from where its steep cliffs met the sea. Grabbing my binoculars from the compartment beside the helm, I did a quick scan of the water and the side of the island, then handed them to Scott.

"No sign of a fire," he said.

I nodded, and we both headed down into the salon. Moving into the main cabin, I entered my closet and opened the safe via the combination lock. I smiled as I looked over all my weapons, which included a Sig Sauer P226 pistol, an HK MP5N submachine gun, and a custom Colt M4A1. It was a little leaner than usual, what with my .338 Lapua sniper rifle and my other Sig being lost, an unfortunate situation which I planned to rectify as soon as possible.

"What's your poison, Scott?" I said and he moved beside me. "It's a small island. Only about three hundred feet at its widest point. It's mostly sloped and covered with palm trees, coconut trees and shrubs in the center. Though I didn't see any extra weapons on his person, there was a shotgun in that helicopter when it went down. So, expect him to be armed with it."

Looking over the contents of my safe for a brief moment, he replied, "I'll take the sub. I know how attached you are to your M4 and Sig."

I handed him the compact submachine gun, then grabbed my extra Sig, strapped the leg holster around my right thigh and checked the magazine to make sure all fifteen rounds were there. Then I snatched the M4 as well, slinging it over my shoulder just in case. Sure, that much firepower was excessive considering Scott and I could probably take him out using only dive knives. But if there was one thing I'd learned in my time in the SEALs, it's that you can never be overprepared for a skirmish.

Moving back up to the deck, we unstrapped the kayak and lowered it into the water. Then I locked up the Baia and grabbed the paddles and we climbed aboard.

# TWENTY-SIX

We paddled quickly over the shallow colorful reef, heading towards the steep cliffs of Monte Cristo. The reef was teeming with life, with a large hogfish, its bright orange body easily visible on the bottom, a school of Spanish mackerel whose silver bodies twinkled in the sunlight, and a vibrant blue tang. I also spotted a handful of lobster, their antennas sticking out of the crevices below.

"I see why we brought the kayak," Scott said, looking over the side at the reef, which was only about three feet beneath the bottom of the plastic at times. Looking forward at the cliffs just a few hundred feet in front of us, he added, "Now if only we had some rock climbing gear."

"We won't need it," I said as I led the way along the cliff, keeping an eye out for any movement on the island.

Scott started to ask me what I meant by that but stopped himself midsentence when he saw the cliffs start to open up, revealing a narrow gap leading towards the center of the island. Paddling only on the right side for a few strokes, I turned us port, then eased us right into the channel.

"Incredible," he said, shaking his head as he looked up at the twenty-foot cliffs rising out of the water on both sides. "I've never seen an island like this in the Keys."

"As far as I know it's the only one," I said, paddling slowly around a small bend. "There's a small lagoon up here, and a beach. Keep your eyes peeled. If he's here, he most likely heard the Baia approach." I kept my voice low and my eyes and ears alert.

As usual, the island was quiet, the only sounds being water splashing softly against the rocks and sand ahead of us and the gentle swaying of palm leaves. Entering the lagoon, I surveyed the palm trees and assorted bushes, searching for any sign of our quarry. We beached the kayak slowly and quietly, stepped out onto the sand and then slid it up a few more feet. Sliding my M4 back over my shoulder, I grabbed my Sig and pulled it out of my leg holster.

As we moved up into the small cluster of rocks, bushes, and trees, Scott veered off to my right flank, keeping about twenty feet of distance between us. The last thing either of us wanted was to be taken by surprise by a guy with a shotgun. A spray of bullets from a shotgun shell could've taken us both down with one shot.

I kept my movements slow and methodical, careful not to make too much noise as I pushed aside a few majesty palm branches and stepped over fallen palm leaves. The effects of Tropical Storm Fay were obvious as there were far more branches and coconuts scattered about the ground than usual. Moving into a small clearing, I held up my fist and knelt down, my eyes catching something unusual in the dirt at my feet. I heard Scott stop as I examined a shoe print that I knew hadn't been left by me when I was there a few days earlier. You could count on one hand the number of living people who knew that there was a lush oasis beyond the cliffs of that island. Judging by the size of the shoe and how fresh the imprint was, I knew that it was Salazar's.

I moved slowly, following a few more prints that led into a thick patch of inkberry bushes and cordgrass under the canopy of low-hanging palm trees. I glanced over at Scott, who was frozen in his tracks to my right, his hands clutching my MP5N. Making eye contact, I motioned towards the patch of bushes. Having stayed on the small island many times before, I knew every inch of it by heart. On the other side of the bushes was the largest flat portion on the island. About a thousand square feet of lush tropical grass where I would usually set up my camp.

As we both stepped through the bushes, we heard footsteps coming from the clearing. I squinted through a patch of ferns and saw Salazar walking with a radio in one hand and a shotgun in the other. He looked terrible. His red button-up shirt and dress pants were covered in dirt and tattered to hell. Even though it had only been a few days, I could tell that he'd lost some weight, and he had patches of black stubble covering his chin. Sitting down under the shade of a palm tree, he brought the radio into his lap and pressed a few buttons.

"Piece of shit," he said, trying the buttons over and over again. Clearly his radio had been damaged when his helicopter had crashed into the sea, which was a good thing for us because it meant he hadn't been able to call in the cavalry.

In his seated position, he was facing away from me, so, glancing over at Scott, I motioned for us to both move in. He circled quietly around to the right, using a portion of a jutting cliff for cover. I went straight for the seated gangster, reaching the clearing in a few seconds and continuing slowly through the grass. When I'd crept to within a few strides of him, he froze suddenly, and I could tell that he'd heard me.

"Don't move," I said, pulling back the metal hammer of my Sig with a loud clink.

I almost squeezed the trigger as he turned his head and looked at me. "Well, holy shit," he said, shaking his head. His voice was raspy, which wasn't surprising since there wasn't a source of fresh water on the island. His only hope would've been whatever was left pooled on the leaves after the heavy rains of Fay. "You're like a damn pest, you know that?" He coughed, glanced at the shotgun lying on the grass just a few inches from his right hand, then added, "I should have killed you when I had the chance."

"Yeah," I said sternly, "you should have. And I mean it, Salazar. You move so much as a muscle towards that shotgun and I'll blow a hole in the back of your head."

He laughed, then grabbed his chest as he coughed once more, this time more violently. "Don't pretend like you won't kill me anyway."

"Kill you?" I said. "No, as much as I'd like to, you're going back into your cage."

"Bullshit!" he yelled.

"He's telling the truth," Scott shouted, appearing from his hiding place behind the trees and jutting cliff. "You're going away, Salazar. Back behind bars.

For life."

Salazar glanced over at Scott, focused his eyes and said, "Is my mind playing tricks, or is that not Senator Cooper?"

"Seriously, Salazar," I said. "Put your hands on your head and stand up, now!" I took a step closer to him and pressed the trigger slightly, ready to fire off a round in the blink of an eye if necessary.

Salazar shook his head, sighed, then stared at the ground. "You know, I made a promise to myself and before God that I would never be caged again. Like my ancestors, I will not go down without a fight."

"You've got three seconds, Salazar!" I barked.

As I started to count down, he said, "*Vaya con Dios*."

In a flash of blurry movement, his right hand jerked for the shotgun and his body dropped forward. He'd just managed to wrap his hand around the wooden handle before Scott and I both pulled the triggers on our weapons, sending bullets exploding into his head from two directions. Blood splattered out from his shattered skull as his body went limp onto the grass. The explosions echoed around the island, and he sat motionless as the smell of gunpowder lingered in the air.

"It's over," I said. I moved in close and examined the disfigured corpse that was all that remained of Benito Salazar.

Scott walked over and stood beside me, hovering over the dead gang leader. "What now?"

"You know me." I did a quick search of his corpse. I found my dive knife strapped to his leg, undid the straps, then slid it into my cargo shorts pocket. Glancing up at Scott, I added, "The last thing I want is to have to deal with law enforcement digging their fingers into all this. And with this guy being such a high-profile target and all, the media would have a field day. Plus, I'd much rather keep this island paradise of mine a secret."

"What are you suggesting?" he said, trying to hold back a smile as best as he could.

Turning my body to face the edge of the cliff at the other side of the clearing, I looked out over the calm blue horizon. As my lips contorted to form a grin, I glanced back at Scott.

He nodded and smiled. "To the locker with him, then."

# TWENTY-SEVEN

Scott and I transported the corpse back to the Baia and then cruised north about half a mile from the reef line, where the depth gauge indicated we were floating on over three hundred feet of water. Tying the metal chain of my spare anchor around Salazar's ankles, we chucked him overboard along with the twenty-pound hunk of aluminum. His body hit the water with a loud splash, then rocketed towards the seafloor, being dragged by the small anchor.

"Bon voyage," I said as he vanished into the darkness of the deep.

While cruising back towards Key West, I couldn't pass up the opportunity to drop beneath the waves a few more times. It was a perfect day, with a slight warm breeze and not a cloud in the sky. Plus, it would be a nice way to get my mind off things and just relax and enjoy the simple things in life.

We dropped anchor near Neptune's Table and free dove the twenty feet to the top of the reef. We spent an hour or so goofing off, weaving in and out of coral and each bagging our limit of lobster. When we were tired and I felt the stitches in my side start to tear, we toweled off, threw the lobster into my live well below the deck and popped open a couple of Paradise Sunset beers. I sprawled out on the sunbed, enjoying the rays of the warm sun as they kissed my bare legs and upper body. Scott was seated on the white cushioned seat beside me, wearing one of those straw Panama hats and staring out into the horizon, admiring the view as much as I was.

"How much longer will you be in town?" I asked after taking a long swig of the smooth brew.

"My flight leaves tomorrow night," he said, leaning back into the cushion. "Just a few hours after the service."

I raised my eyebrows and glanced over at him. "Service?"

"Yeah, there's a memorial service tomorrow at Key West Cemetery for the three Coast Guardsmen that lost their lives during that helicopter crash."

I sat in silence a moment. I couldn't help but replay the incident over again in my head, as I had many times since it had happened. "I should never have made that distress call," I said, shaking my head as I stared out over the turquoise water. "The damn radio died before I could warn them about the gang members and that ship." I took in a deep breath, then sighed. "It's my fa—"

"Don't you dare finish that sentence," he said, sitting up. He pulled his sunglasses from his face and stared me in the eyes. "What happened to those guys wasn't your fault. You hear me? You were a bigger man than most for getting involved, and for saving that family's life. Don't you get it? Those girls will grow up now because of you. That couple will grow old together. They will see their daughters get married and have a future. You did that, Logan. And as far as the distress call goes, you only did what any other man with a good head on his shoulders would've done." Then, looking out over the horizon, he took in a deep breath and stared back at me. "It wasn't your fault."

It was hard for me to believe, but his words had caused my eyes to water and I had to look away. I wasn't one to cry very often. In fact, I hadn't cried for two years. Not since I'd found out my dad had died.

He leaned back into his chair, slid his sunglasses back over his ears and added, "And if I ever hear you say that kind of bullshit ever again, I'll kick your ass, you hear me?"

I smiled, then stood up and placed a hand on his shoulder. "Thanks, Scott. You want another cold one?"

"You're reading my mind, brother."

A few hours later, we pulled the Baia back into my slip in Conch Marina, tied her off, and locked her up, and then Scott drove me back to the hospital. We'd both grabbed a quick shower on the boat and cleaned off as well as we could. I decided against wearing Ted's maintenance uniform for a second round and slipped into the back door of the hospital wearing my normal attire of a tee shirt, cargo shorts, and flip-flops. As Scott dropped me off, I told him that I'd see him the following day at the memorial service.

Slipping back into my room with just a few glances from passing nurses, I changed out of my clothes and back into the hospital gown, which, though embarrassing as hell, was actually pretty comfortable. Climbing back onto the bed, I pulled the covers over me and dropped my head into the soft pillow.

"Where have you been?" a voice said from the door, and as I turned, I realized it was the young, freckle-faced deputy Wilkes had left to watch over me.

"The Coral Sea," I replied with a grin. He looked at me, confused, and shook his head. "Forget it," I added, realizing that my reference to the old Navy cadence had gone about a mile over his head.

As I reached for the bottle of water on the tray beside the bed, he stepped closer to me and looked at me as if he were a parent who'd caught their teenager sneaking out past curfew.

After a few awkward moments of him staring at me, I said, "What?"

He sighed. "You weren't supposed to leave the hospital, Mr. Dodge. Where did you go, anyway?"

I smiled and said, "Just took a quick swim over near Fort Zachary Taylor. Swimming is great for rehab."

"Why didn't you tell anyone? You're supposed to check out with the staff, you know."

"Look, I've been away from government work for almost six years now. I'm not exactly in the habit of telling people where I'm going and when. Plus, last I checked, this is a free country we live in. I can stay or go as I please. Now, would you mind shutting the door when you leave? I really should be getting some rest."

I grinned as he turned on his heel and walked with heavy, defeated steps out the door, shutting it sternly behind him. I spent most of the evening scarfing down hospital food that surprisingly wasn't half-bad and watching Jason Bourne beat up bad guys on HBO. My body was still in pretty bad shape, and the long day out on the water had made me exhausted, making me pop down a few pain relievers and call it a night at 2100.

The following day, I'd had all I could take and checked myself out before breakfast. Carrying a bag of prescription drugs in one hand, I stepped through the automatic front doors and saw Jack sitting in the driver's seat of his blue Jeep Wrangler with the top down. I'd called him about fifteen minutes earlier using the hospital phone.

"Damn good to see you, bro," he said. Then, looking at the marks on my face and seeing the way I walked, careful not to put too much weight on my right leg, he added, "Did they recommend that you leave, or is this you?"

"Little of both. But mostly me." I chuckled and Jack smiled.

We talked briefly about what had happened the past few days, me telling him about fighting off Salazar's goons on Loggerhead and him telling me about Fay and the damage she'd caused. When we turned onto Palmetto Street, he said, "Say, are you going to the service this afternoon? It's five o'clock at Key West Cemetery."

"I'll be there," I said. The truth was, I'd never much liked funerals. I mean, I guess nobody really does. But I wanted nothing more than to show those guys as much respect as I could for what they'd done.

A minute later, he turned past the black mailbox with the number 38 stenciled in white letters and onto the brick driveway leading to my house. I was surprised to see that there didn't appear to be much damage to my house and property. A few fallen branches and knocked-over potted plants, but beyond that, it was hard to tell that a storm had even blown through. I even spotted my black Tacoma parked under the house, which explained why I hadn't seen it at the marina the previous day.

"I did what I could to stormproof the place, and I moved your truck. Under your house is much more protected than over at the marina parking lot," he said, observing me as I surveyed the property. I thanked him earnestly as I opened the passenger-side door. "Look," he added, leaning towards me, "you want me to stick around here for a few hours? I've got a charter scheduled to leave at ten, but I can cancel it."

I waved a hand in the air. "I'm fine." Then I shut the door and leaned in the window. "Thanks for the ride. I'll see you this afternoon."

"You got it, bro," he said, smiling at me as he put the Jeep in gear and backed out.

I did a walk about my property, which didn't take long considering I only had about a quarter acre and a little over a hundred feet of waterfront on the channel. There'd been little to no damage to the house itself. A few shingles had blown off, and a few of my security cameras and motion sensors had been damaged, but that was about it. One of the reasons I'd purchased this house in the first place was because of its design, which made it well suited for surviving even the most powerful tropical storms.

I spent the rest of the morning and early afternoon cleaning up the palm leaves and working around the house. Before lunch, I did a quick forty-five-minute low-impact workout consisting of mainly resistance bands and body weight exercises. Then I feasted on a few lobsters Scott had cooked up and left in my cooler and relaxed in the hammock strung out on my patio, facing the waterway.

# TWENTY-EIGHT

Later that afternoon, I showered, shaved and put on the best and only suit I owned, then drove my Tacoma over to the cemetery. The entire incident, and especially the Coast Guard helicopter being blown out of the sky, had made national headlines. The president himself had made a formal address regarding the issue and had ordered the national ensign to be flown at half-mast for three days in their honor. Though he couldn't make it to the ceremony himself, there were a handful of political representatives present, including Scott and the governor of Florida, Joyce Richardson.

I stood beside Jack and his fifteen-year-old nephew, Isaac, in the shade of a large gumbo-limbo tree near the back of the massive group that huddled around the three black caskets. The truth was I'd only been to two other funerals before. Once for my mom, who'd passed away from cancer when I was eight years old, and the other for one of my Navy brothers we'd lost when our platoon was ambushed on a reconnaissance mission in Colombia.

This ceremony was similar to the one for the lost hero, with American flags spread out over the caskets and a row of uniformed soldiers firing off three volleys. The governor gave a quick speech, praising their courage and the sacrifices they'd made, along with two other politicians, including Scott.

At the front of the group, I saw a young woman in a black dress holding a newborn baby in her arms. She had a difficult time standing as tears streaked down her face. I knew that it was Anne, Ryan's widow, and his son. As the bugler played taps and an admiral presented her with a folded flag, she almost lost it completely.

When the ceremony finished, I tried to get close enough to talk to her, but she was surrounded by a group of friends, family, politicians, and uniformed service members, each offering their deepest sympathies for what had happened to her husband. Deciding it wasn't the best time, I headed for the parking lot alongside Jack and Isaac.

As I slid my key into the driver's-side door, I heard a voice calling my name softly. Turning around, I saw Harper Ridley walking towards me, weaving around the cars that filled the edge of the parking lot.

"Logan," she said, stepping right up to my open driver's-side window. She was wearing a black dress along with a black hat with white edging.

Harper had been a writer for the *Keynoter* since I was young, and even though she was now well into her forties, she didn't look it. She had long dark hair that she usually kept pulled back, and she somehow managed to have pale skin, even while living so close to the equator. More than anything else, though, I think it was the ease and lightness of her feet as she moved around that made her look younger than her years.

"I'd like to meet with you sometime this week. It's not every day I get to write such a heroic piece."

"Those are the real heroes," I said, motioning towards the gravesites. "Not me. Any story you write should be about them and how they sacrificed their lives in order to save a group of strangers."

She smiled softly. "Yes, well, I would still like to hear your side of things. That is, if you're willing."

I thought about it for a second, then said, "Meet me at Pete's for lunch around noon tomorrow."

Then I pulled out of the cemetery parking lot and headed over to the marina, where Jack and I had dinner on the Baia with Scott before he had to fly back up to Washington. We feasted on the fresh lobster Scott and I had hauled in the previous day, dousing the succulent tails in Swamp Sauce with a squeeze of fresh lemon juice. When we finished eating, he drove his black rental SUV to Key West International Airport, and Jack and I sat for a few hours more, watching as the sun dropped down below the distant horizon. There's something about a Florida Keys sunset that never gets old. It manages to take my breath away each and every time.

I passed out on the boat and woke up the next morning naturally just after six. After a quick breakfast of mango, banana and a bowl of Grape-Nuts, I downed a mug of coffee, then drove my Tacoma back to my house to make a few more repairs to the outside. It only took a few hours, and afterward I started what I'd intended to be an easy five-mile run, but it turned into more of a mile walk and jog.

My leg and side both still hurt pretty bad, but I knew that in a few months, I'd be back in the game.

At noon, I met Harper at Salty Pete's and we ate lunch on the second-story patio. I tried my best to relate to her all the events as they'd occurred, but left out a few of the gory details, not wanting to spoil her appetite. Pete brought us out fresh hogfish that he'd caught just that morning, and as usual Oz had done a superb job with the cooking, blackening the fish to perfection.

Once she'd gotten what she needed for her story, I reached for my wallet. "It's on the house," Pete said, contorting his dark, leathery skin into a smile.

We both thanked him, then parted ways. When I hopped back into my Tacoma, I knew what I had to do, though it was the last thing I wanted to do. Glancing at my new smartphone, I saw the three voicemails left in the past twenty-four hours from the Key West police office's main number. Putting the truck in gear, I pulled out and headed over to the police station.

For the most part, the ordeal was just long and boring, and if it hadn't been for the constant supply of coffee, I doubt I would have made it. But at one point, one of the officers, while taking part of my statement, really rubbed me the wrong way when he said, "You know, you racked up quite the body count on that island." He was a pretty young guy, maybe about my age, and he had a know-it-all air about him. "Do you really think it was all necessary?"

Shooting him a stern look, I said, "Every single one of those bastards was trying to kill me and that family, and they almost succeeded. What would you have had me do, asked them politely to lower their weapons?" I shook my head. "If I had, there would have been eight caskets at that funeral yesterday." Then I leaned back in my chair, never once looking away from the officer's eyes. "No, deadly force was not only justified but necessary considering the circumstances." That shut him up pretty good, and fortunately, he was the only officer in the department who felt that way, and even he had a change of heart and apologized by the time I stood up to leave.

After four and a half grueling hours of writing and answering question after question, Wilkes patted me on the shoulder and said that they'd gotten everything they needed and that he would be in contact with me if anything else came up.

"You know," he said as he walked me through the front door of the police station, "I spoke to Dave Tillman, the owner of that shrimping boat, the *Jean Louise*, and he said he saw your boat cruising out past Dry Tortugas yesterday." Then he grinned at me and added, "That's a long way from Fort Zachary Taylor."

I smiled back at him and patted him on the shoulder. "I think that old sea dog needs to get his eyes checked. I'll see you around, Sheriff."

"Hey, Logan," he said before I reached the door of my Tacoma. Stepping closer to me, he said, "I know you and I don't know each other too well yet. But please, call me Charles."

I gave him a slow and friendly nod. "Okay, Charles," I said, feeling like we were finally getting to know each other's character, at least a little bit. As he turned around, I remembered that I'd wanted to ask him something and thought that now was an appropriate time. "Say, do you think you could tell me where Anne Cody lives? I wanted to speak with her yesterday but figured I should wait."

"Sure," he replied. "She's renting one of the cottages over on Mangrove Street. Hers is number four."

I thanked him, then hopped into the driver's seat, started up the engine and pulled out of the lot. On my way over to Anne's cottage, I made a quick stop at Flowers by Gilda and bought a large bouquet of assorted flowers, which included pink roses, purple iris, blue hydrangea, white orchids and orange snapdragons with their stems in a fancy crystal vase. When I turned onto Mangrove Street, I saw the cottages Charles had been referring to, lined up in a row along the street.

Parking my truck against the curb, I grabbed the flowers and walked along the sidewalk until I saw the number four stenciled on the side of a cottage in white paint. The cottages were nice, each painted sky blue, with white picket fences surrounding their small front yards. As I stepped towards the front porch of Anne's cottage, I tried to think about what I should say. I'd hoped that the right words would come to me during the drive over, but they hadn't.

Holding the bouquet in my right hand, I pressed my finger against the small button beside the door and heard the doorbell ring inside. I waited for about fifteen seconds, then, having not heard any movement inside, I turned around, set the bouquet on the top of the stairs and headed back towards my truck. When I reached the bottom step of her front porch, I heard the door open behind me. Turning around, I saw Anne standing in the doorway, staring at me behind the screen door. She was wearing sweatpants and a gray tee shirt, and she looked like she'd just woken up.

"Yes?" she said softly as we made eye contact. Then she glanced down at the flowers, wiped the bottom of her nose and added, “Thank you.” Slowly, I went up the stairs and stood a few feet away from her on the other side of the screen. “I’m sorry, I’m afraid I don’t recognize you. Did you know Ryan?”

My heart started to pound rapidly in my chest. I calmed myself, taking in a slow breath and said, “Yes, ma’am. I… I was on the island when he crashed.”

Her eyes grew wide as she stared into mine, hearing the seriousness in my voice. “You must be Logan. He spoke about you before. Said he met you in the Everglades.”

I nodded. “Yeah. Look, for whatever it’s worth, ma’am—”

She shook her head and held up a finger. “Call me Anne.”

“Right. For whatever it’s worth, Anne, I’m very sorry for what happened.”

She waved a hand at me. “No. Don’t be sorry, Logan. He did his job, and what happened was nobody’s fault but those damn gang members.” She paused a moment, and I saw her eyes start to water. “The news stations say that the hunt is still on for the man responsible.”

“Don’t worry about him,” I said, and without thinking I added, “He’s hundreds of feet beneath the waves and probably eaten to nothing but bare bones by now.”

Her eyes narrowed and her mouth dropped open. “You? You killed him?”

I nodded. “I’d appreciate it if you kept that between us.”

She smiled faintly. “I understand.”

Glancing into the house, I said, “Are you planning to stay in Key West for long?”

"No," she said, shaking her head. "We're heading back to Colorado. It's where Ryan and I are from. It's where we grew up and went to high school together. He always wanted to serve. He'd wanted to join the Army, but bless his heart, I'd talked him out of it. I never wanted him to be in danger, so we compromised and he joined the Coast Guard." Her eyes filled up with tears, and she buried her face in her hands. "I never thought that…" She struggled with the words. "I never thought something like this would happen."

"I'm so sorry, Anne," I said, pulling open the screen door and wrapping an arm around her.

After a few moments of crying, she wiped her face with the backs of her hands and sniffled a few times.

"Anne," I said, looking into her eyes, "I was with Ryan when he died, and he wanted me to tell you that he loved you very much. He also asked me to look after your son for him. I'm not talking about just monetarily either, though I'll be sending checks whether you like it or not. I'm talking about being there for him or for you if you ever need anything."

I gave her a hug, then loosened my grip and headed back towards the stairs. "Thank you, Logan," she said before I reached the top step. "And I'm not just talking about for the flowers either."

Turning back, I looked at her and smiled. "Your husband was a great man. He would want you to be strong. Whatever you do, don't give up. No matter how hard it gets, you never give up, alright?"

She closed her eyes, nodding at me as I turned back around and headed for my Tacoma.

# TWENTY-NINE

I spent the next few weeks hanging out around town with Jack, helping him with the occasional charter, and going out diving and exploring the islands just about every day. My workout regimen, which had been thrown out of whack by my injuries, was starting to amp up again. I felt my body healing itself as I gradually increased the intensity and duration of my workouts and spent more time than usual stretching and icing my muscles. It wasn't long before I could run the full eight-mile loop from my house that started south and circled around Fort Zachary Taylor along the waterfront before passing the Conch Marina and finishing back at my house.

Three weeks after the incident in Dry Tortugas, I received a large manila envelope addressed from the Hale family in Miami. I was surprised to see it, since I hadn't spoken to any of them since that morning on Loggerhead. Inside the envelope, I found a small stack of letters written to me by various members of the family. They each had their own unique flair, and they each thanked me for what I'd done and hoped that I was recovering well. Cynthia wrote me a note explaining how Alex had been assigned a school project to write a paper and do a presentation on someone that she admired, and she'd chosen me. I smiled as I read her paper, which even included a pretty good sketch of me standing in front of the lighthouse back on the island.

Chris wrote saying that if I ever needed anything, whether legal help or personal help, he'd do whatever he could. But it was Cynthia's letter, which consisted of two lined pages with writing on both sides of the paper, that caused me to sit down on my couch and feel the most emotion. She explained how great she thought I was and how she admired me in so many ways. She thanked me from the bottom of her heart for saving her family and wrote that she knew that there was no way she'd ever be able to repay me. As I read her words, I thought about her—how well she'd handled herself, how she'd saved my life and how beautiful she was. I couldn't help but think about how our lives might've been if we'd met each other as single adults. But I pushed those thoughts aside and stood up from the couch. I had a strict no-married-women policy that I was proud to have adhered to my entire life, and I wasn't looking to break it now, or ever.

Moving into the kitchen, I stuck a few of the letters, as well as Alex's sketch, onto the refrigerator using a couple of *I Love Key West* magnets that were there when I'd bought the place. Then I spent the next couple of days out on the water, enjoying the tropical paradise that I called home and spending my days diving, spearfishing and island hopping and my evenings out with Jack.

Pulling into my driveway after hanging out and drinking at Pete's place with Jack, Pete, and Gus one night, I walked up the steps to the side door of my house and dropped my keys as I fished them out of my front pocket. As I bent down to pick them up, I noticed that the small black cable leading into one of the motion sensors on my porch had been tampered with. As I moved in and examined it closer, I realized that someone had cut the cable on the small section between where it connected to the sensor and disappeared into the house.

I reached for my Sig instinctively, sliding it free from its concealed position around my waist and under my shirt. My breathing slow and controlled, I ran scenarios through my head, thinking of a plan. Rising slowly from my crouched position, I peered in through the side windows. There were no lights on inside the house and no noise or movement of any kind. But someone was there. I could feel it. Someone was in my house, and whoever they were, they were very good. Clearly a skilled assassin. Perhaps it was someone still loyal to Salazar. Or maybe Black Venom had hired a guy to come and take me out. Fortunately, I'd happened to drop my keys and notice what they'd done to my motion sensor. If I hadn't, I would have probably walked right into a bullet.

I moved around the porch, keeping my body low and my steps quiet as I surveyed the inside of the house. It was useless. I couldn't see a thing in the darkness.

Moving for the back door, I slowly stuck my key into the hole and unlocked it. Aiming my Sig chest height, I pushed it open, stepped through the doorway and flipped on the living room lights.

"Don't shoot, Logan," a female voice said coolly and casually. It was a voice I'd recognize anywhere, I thought as Angelina turned her head to look at me. At first glance, Angelina Fox looked like one of those women you'd see in the Swimsuit Edition of *Sports Illustrated*. At five foot ten and with long, sexy blond hair, sparkling blue eyes and the tan, lean body of a triathlete, she was sure to turn heads wherever she went. But beneath her easy-on-the-eyes appearance was a badass warrior who'd fought in the Brazilian Special Operations Command, the first woman ever to do so, and was also one of the deadliest mercenaries in the world. We'd been friends, with occasional benefits, ever since we'd both started out as guns for hire, and she'd saved my butt on more than one occasion.

As I stood across the living room from her, my facial expression contorting from focused to a grin that stretched from ear to ear, she continued, "I heard you had quite the scare during Fay. Could it be that Logan Dodge finally met his match?"

"What kind of crazy person would ever give you an idea like that?" I said, sliding my Sig back into my waist, then walking in front of her and placing my hands on my hips.

"Harper Ridley," she said. Then, leaning forward on the couch, she reached for a folded-up newspaper on the table in front of her. "Says here you were inches from death."

"What the hell?" I said, grabbing the paper from her hands. After taking a second to read the first paragraph, I shook my head. "Shit, this isn't what I told her."

Ange chuckled as she pointed at the date printed into the top right corner of the *Keynoter*. "This is from last week. Don't you ever read the newspaper down here? Hell, I don't even live in the Keys, and I feel like I've read it more times than you."

"I glance at it from time to time," I said with my most charming smile. "Granted, it's only when I have a fish to wrap."

She laughed, and I sat down beside her and kissed her on the cheek, noticing that she smelled really good. Glancing at my dive watch, I saw that it was after eleven at night, and I could feel my stomach rumble when I realized that I hadn't eaten since lunch.

Looking into her fiery blue eyes, I said, "Hungry?"

"You read my mind. I've been flying for the last two and half hours from Nassau and I'm starving."

Ange and I had actually gotten our pilot's licenses together a few years ago. But she had taken a liking to it more than I had and continued to pursue more advanced training.

"Is your plane over at Key West International?"

She smiled and shook her head. "Tarpon Cove Marina. It's a seaplane."

We moved outside onto the patio, and I cooked up four lobster tails from bugs that I'd kept in a sixty-gallon holding tank. Then, grabbing my bucket of clams, I boiled up about two dozen of them and we feasted, enjoying the fresh seafood and washing it down with a couple of margaritas. It was a nice evening, warm and with a slight breeze coming over the channel from the ocean beyond. When we finished, I plopped into my hammock and Ange sat beside me on one of my cushioned wicker chairs. She grabbed a skinny leather pouch from the table out of curiosity and pulled out a sharpened silver throwing knife.

"I've got a small target on the trunk of that palm tree over there," I said, motioning to the target about thirty feet away from us. She smiled and nodded as she examined the blade closely.

After a moment's pause, she said, "You remember that day at Pete's? When there was that big party to celebrate finding the Aztec treasure?" Before I'd replied, she continued, "Well, there was something that I wanted to tell you that day but couldn't bring myself to."

My eyes grew wide. "What's that, Ange?"

"It's about Sam," she said. "I didn't see her as your type."

I smiled and realized that I hadn't thought about her since I'd been on Loggerhead. "Oh, really?"

"Yeah," she said as she grabbed her margarita and killed the rest of it with a few big gulps. Playing with the knife in her hands, she spun it a few times, then gripped the handle, reared it back and flung it in the direction of the target with a strong flick of her wrist. The blade flew through the air so fast that all I could see was a metallic blur until it stabbed straight into the center of my makeshift wooden target. Glancing over at me, she added, "She wasn't dangerous enough for you."

After finishing the pitcher of margarita, we were unable to keep our hands off each other as we stumbled into the master bedroom. I've had my share of lovers in the past and enjoyed the company of beautiful women as much as any man does. But that night seemed to stand out above the rest as we lay in each other's arms, our sweat-covered bodies calling it quits just as the first rays of sunlight peeked over the horizon and bled through the thin curtains covering my bedroom window.

I woke up on my back with Ange sprawled out beside me, her arm draped over me and her head resting softly against my chest. Seeing that it was past noon and unable to believe that I'd slept in so long, I slowly crawled out of bed, kissing Ange on the forehead before heading into the living room. I made a pot of coffee and cut into a couple of mangoes and a banana. I'd never really been one to eat a heavy breakfast, but after going all night, I felt like my body needed it, so I also cooked up some eggs and pancakes. As the smell of coffee and warm hotcakes filled the air, Ange appeared, moving with light feet into the kitchen and wearing nothing but one of my old tee shirts. Somehow, she managed to look amazing even in the morning with her blond hair a mess.

It was well over eighty degrees outside, so we enjoyed breakfast at the dining table, which still had a pretty good view of my backyard and the narrow channel where my twenty-two-foot Robalo center-console was stored. After breakfast, we showered together, then got dressed and headed over to the marina, where we took the Baia out for an afternoon on the water.

"Finally named her, huh?" Ange had said, glancing at the black letters stenciled onto the transom as we'd climbed aboard. About a week after getting out of the hospital, Jack had hooked me up with a guy who was able to come out and paint the name on that same day. "*Dodging Bullets*," she added. "I like it."

After cruising around the Lower Keys for an hour, we anchored down between Looe Key and American Shoal, just southwest of Big Pine Key, then donned scuba gear and dropped beneath the waves. It had been years since I'd dived the *Adolphus Busche* wreck, which was a 210-foot freighter that had been intentionally sunk back in 1998. Descending seventy feet and hovering just over the main deck, I scanned over the ship and was amazed at how well the ocean had transformed it into an artificial reef in just the ten years since it had been scuttled.

The ship was teeming at every corner with colorful marine life, including stingrays, lemon sharks and a massive school of silversides. Finning into the cargo holds, we spotted two resident goliath grouper, one of which looked to be over five hundred pounds. Moving out and along the ship's hull, we peered into the portholes and saw a few green moray eels swimming mystically in place and staring back at us.

When the oxygen in our tanks started to run low, we headed back up to the surface and relaxed on the sunbed together, watching as the sun dropped down in the western sky.

A week later, as we were lounging in my hammock on the upstairs patio of my house, Ange turned to me and said, "You know, I think I'd like to have a fancy dinner tonight. How does Latitudes sound?"

I smiled. "That sounds great."

Latitudes was one of the nicest restaurants in the Keys, and it was world famous because it was located on a small island just off Key West. Usually, guests hopped aboard a small ferry that shuttled wealthy tourists wearing fancy suits and dresses over to the restaurant. But after we got all dressed up, I chose to take us over in style, mooring the Baia on the small private dock right beside the restaurant.

After walking past a row of fountains and

beautiful flowers, we entered through the large double glass doors, and Ange surprised me when she told the hostess that she had a reservation for two.

"I made it last week," she said, smiling at me as we were ushered over to our table. She was wearing a sexy blue dress and, combined with her diamond earrings and high-heeled shoes, she looked like she'd just walked out of a photoshoot for some high-end fashion magazine.

The hostess led us to a table right beside a large window that overlooked the ocean, and I helped Ange into her chair before seating myself. Before the hostess could ask what we wanted to drink, Ange said, "We'll have a tequila sunrise and a classic mojito, please." She smiled at me, and I thought that I sure as hell could get used to this.

I couldn't help but grin as Ange sat with her back straight and her arms placed formally at her sides. During a late-night talk we'd had a few years earlier, she'd told me that her parents had put her into the best boarding schools when she was a young girl growing up in Sweden. She'd said that they'd been grooming her to be a rich man's wife and hang around at country clubs for the rest of her life. And even though she'd always been a bit of a tomboy and had done everything she could to resist it, she had a hard time hiding the back straight, formal dining habits she'd been forced to adopt as a young girl.

For appetizers, we ordered the lobster bisque and the carpaccio of beef; both were incredible, and the bisque was the best I'd ever tasted. For dinner, Ange decided on the seafood pasta, which had jumbo shrimp, seared scallops and lobster combined with seasonings and fresh tagliatelle pasta. I chose the yellowtail snapper with sweet baby peppers and chive risotto.

When the waitress brought our food over, my mouth watered as all of the different aromas swirled into my nostrils. It was some of the best seafood I had ever had, and as we talked, Ange told me about how the owner was a world-renowned chef who'd fallen in love with the Keys when he'd visited there years earlier.

As I enjoyed each bite and looked across at Ange, admiring her beauty, I felt like I'd died and gone to heaven.

"You know, I'm one lucky guy," I said, admiring her.

She nodded. "Yeah. With all those gang members hunting you down on that island, you'd think one of them would've been able to bring you down. Maybe the Keys aren't making you soft after all."

"I'm in the best shape of my life," I replied confidently.

"Is that so?" she said, eyeing me from head to toe. "Well, if that's the case, maybe you could actually give me a run for my money in a fight now."

"You and I both know you'd beat me up," I said, grinning at her. She laughed and nodded as I continued, "But I wasn't referring to that. I meant that I'm lucky to be dining with such a beautiful and intelligent woman as you." She blushed a little bit but tried her best to brush it off.

When we were about halfway through eating our main courses, I saw a familiar face approach our table from the direction of the front door. It was Sheriff Wilkes, though he wasn't dressed in his uniform. Instead, he was wearing blue jeans and a button-up Hawaiian-style shirt. I was surprised they'd let him in.

"Logan," he said, stepping right up to the table.

"Hey, Charles," I said, smiling at him. "Little underdressed, aren't we?" My smile died as I saw the serious look on his face.

"I've been looking for you everywhere," he said. Then, glancing at Ange, he added, "Can I speak to you in private?"

I apologized to Ange, who seemed more intrigued than anything else, then sighed, set my napkin on the table and walked alongside him towards the waiting area and through the front doors.

Once we were outside and out of earshot of everyone except a few nicely dressed tourists walking down the path towards the ferry, I turned to face him. "Look, I've already told you everything," I said, irritated that he'd interrupted my meal with Ange. "I've given my full statement more times than I can count. I've played ball with you guys, and for the last time, I don't know where Salazar is." It wasn't completely a lie. I mean, sure, I knew his general whereabouts, but I didn't know his exact location. I hadn't even looked at the coordinates of my GPS when we'd chucked him overboard.

"It's not that," he said, his face emotionless. "You have a message from a detective down in Curacao. He said he's been trying to get a hold of you all day."

"A detective in Curacao?" I said, confused as hell. "What's the message?"

"To call him right away," he said, handing me a slip of paper with a phone number penned onto it. "He couldn't tell me anything, but he said it's important, Logan."

I stood for a moment, wondering why in the hell

a detective from Curacao would have urgent business with me, then grabbed the slip of paper and held my hand out. “Mind if I borrow your phone? Mine fell into the ocean.”

“Explains why I couldn’t get ahold of you,” he said as he handed it to me and I punched in the numbers. After the second ring, I heard a guy’s voice through the small speaker.

“Hello?” the loud voice said in what sounded like a Spanish accent.

“This is Logan Dodge calling from Key West, Florida,” I said. “Sheriff Charles Wilkes has just informed me that you’ve been trying to get ahold of me.”

I heard shuffling of papers on the other end of the phone. “Yes, Mr. Dodge, this is Detective Dan Millis of the Curacao Police Department.” There was a slight pause, and I listened intently as he took a deep breath, then let it out. “Look, I’m sorry, but I have some bad news for you.”

“Bad news?” I said, wondering what in the hell he could possibly be talking about.

“Yes, sir. It’s about your father.” My eyes grew wide and my heart stopped at the mention of my dad.

“What about him?” The words jumped angrily out of my mouth. My mind raced wildly, wondering what could have happened.

“Look—uh, it’s of a serious nature, and I’d rather not discuss it over the phone.”

“What happened?” I said again, my voice loud and stern.

He sighed. “It’s regarding your father’s gravesite.”

My dad’s gravesite? My blood boiled and I gritted my teeth, unable to control my anger.

"Go on," I said.

"I don't know how to tell you this, Mr. Dodge, but it's been desecrated." That sent me overboard, sending a surge of burning hot rage through my body. Who in the hell would desecrate my dad's body? And why? He cleared his throat and continued, "I know this must be tough to hear. Is there any chance you could make it down here to the island sometime in the next couple of days?"

"I'll be there in the morning," I said in a pissed-off tone, then hung up the phone and handed it back to Charles, who was staring at me intently.

"What was that about?" he asked, trying his best to read me.

I stared off into the distance, lost in thought and breathing heavily. I didn't know who in the hell would ever do such a thing, but I did know one thing for certain: whoever was responsible was going to pay.

"I'm going to be out of town for a few days," I said, still staring off into nothingness.

In a moment, my life had been turned upside down. I glanced over at Ange, who was waiting patiently for me at our table, and knew that I had no choice but to cut our time in paradise short.

# THE END

**Logan Dodge Adventures**

Gold in the Keys
(Florida Keys Adventure Series Book 1)

Hunted in the Keys
(Florida Keys Adventure Series Book 2)

Revenge in the Keys
(Florida Keys Adventure Series Book 3)

Betrayed in the Keys
(Florida Keys Adventure Series Book 4)

Redemption in the Keys
(Florida Keys Adventure Series Book 5)

If you'd like to receive my newsletter to get updates on upcoming books and special deals, you can sign up on my website:

matthewrief.com

# About the Author

Matthew has a deep-rooted love for adventure and the ocean. He loves traveling, diving, rock climbing and writing adventure novels. Though he grew up in the Pacific Northwest, he currently lives in Virginia Beach with his wife, Jenny.

Made in United States
Orlando, FL
01 May 2025